How could any twenty-first-century man *believe* this stuff?

As April continued to read the manuscript, making notations in the margin, she had to bite her lip to keep from laughing.

"So, you're working on 'The Mating Game' article," a familiar voice broke in.

She looked up at Thomas Eldridge, the magazine's publisher and editor in chief. To her chagrin, he wasn't alone.

"Sorry," she said. "I'm afraid I was busy reading this unbelievable submission. To tell you the truth, I was trying not to laugh."

"Laugh?" Tom said with a warning frown. "Well, if you think you can contain yourself, I'd like to introduce you to Lucas Sullivan—the author of this piece."

Before she could apologize, Tom went on. "Sullivan here is a noted sociologist. The article you have is one I asked him to write."

April turned to smile at Lucas Sullivan. At first glance he looked like the stereotypical absentminded professor—a thatch of unruly brown hair, clothes a little rumpled, smelling ever so slightly of musty old books.

But on second glance... Under that staid exterior was one very sexy male.

Dear Reader,

You might be interested to know that when I was plotting my trilogy SULLIVAN'S RULES I discovered I was actually incorporating my own life into the three stories.

As in this book, April Morgan's story, my own young dream was to marry a man who would treat me as an equal.

The second book, coming in December of this year, is about April's friend Rita Rosales. There—as in my own life—the hero turns out to be the boy next door. We had two children and twenty-three wonderful years together before I lost him.

As in the third book, Lili Soule's story, I was given a second chance at finding the strong yet gentle man who became my husband.

Like the three women in my stories, I believe in love and a happy-ever-after. That's why I love writing stories of home, heart and happiness for Harlequin American Romance.

I hope you enjoy reading about April, Rita and Lili as much as I enjoyed writing about them!

Mollie Molay

Books by Mollie Molay

HARLEQUIN AMERICAN ROMANCE

938—THE DUCHESS & HER BODYGUARD*
947—SECRET SERVICE DAD*
954—COMMANDER'S LITTLE SURPRISE*
987—MY BIG FAKE GREEN-CARD WEDDING

*Grooms in Uniform

MARRIAGE IN SIX EASY LESSONS

Mollie Molay

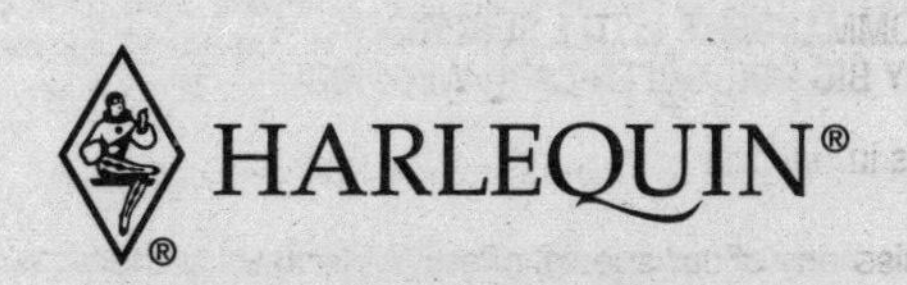

TORONTO • NEW YORK • LONDON
AMSTERDAM • PARIS • SYDNEY • HAMBURG
STOCKHOLM • ATHENS • TOKYO • MILAN • MADRID
PRAGUE • WARSAW • BUDAPEST • AUCKLAND

ISBN 0-373-75027-7

MARRIAGE IN SIX EASY LESSONS

This edition published by arrangement with Harlequin Books S.A.

www.eHarlequin.com

Printed in U.S.A.

To newcomers Joseph Murray Fox and Luke Joseph Molé.
Welcome to the world.

Sullivan's Rules

1. A happy relationship requires that a woman make her man feel masculine.
2. While a man is not monogamous by nature, he is more likely to see a woman as a potential girlfriend or mate if sexual intimacy doesn't occur too soon.
3. A woman must rein in her own desires to promote the health of a relationship.
4. A woman must strive for compatibility, rather than try to be sexy.
5. A woman must show her man how much she likes and appreciates him. She must shower him with affection and sublimate her own daily frustrations.
6. A woman must be supportive, fun-loving, easygoing and generous in her praise of a man's achievements.

Prologue

A few last-minute guests at the Morgan-Blair wedding hurried to take their seats in the flower-decorated nave of St. James Church-by-the-Lake. The church organist launched into the romantic and emotional "Lara's Theme" from *Dr. Zhivago,* a prearranged signal that the wedding ceremony would begin in twenty minutes.

In the bride's dressing room, the bride, April Morgan, frowned and regarded her bridal bouquet of white roses and gardenias with a growing sense of unease.

Rita Rosales, her maid of honor, tucked something borrowed, a tiny good-luck charm, in April's shoe. "There, that should take care of the wedding ceremony." She laughed as she adjusted the shoulder straps of her pale green dress. "The honeymoon is up to you."

April's face whitened.

"Now, Rita," Lili Soulé, the matron of honor, scolded, "April doesn't need any of your teasing.

Can't you see she's already nervous?'' She checked the basket of flowers that the little maid of honor, her daughter Paulette, was carrying to make sure the rose petals were still inside. Paul, the ring bearer and Paulette's twin brother, clutched the satin cushion holding the wedding rings to his chest.

''I'm okay,'' April murmured, although she was becoming more nervous by the minute. ''Rita, why don't you see if any of the bridesmaids need help before the ceremony?''

Rita glanced over to where the bridesmaids were busy checking their gowns in floor-length mirrors. ''There doesn't seem to be a problem. All five of them are looking good.''

April's frown deepened. ''Five? There's supposed to be six!'' She scanned the group uneasily. ''Where's Claire Dunn?'' she called to them.

''Claire just stepped outside for a minute,'' Joyce Humphries called back.

''Did she say she's going to get back in here in time for the ceremony?''

Joyce shrugged and turned back to the floor-length mirror. ''Claire is Claire. Who knows what she's going to do next?''

Aware of Claire Dunn's erratic behavior lately, April tried not to think that the bridesmaid's disappearance was a bad omen.

She dismissed the growing hollow feeling in her middle as a case of prewedding jitters, but deep in her heart she knew there was more to her growing unease. The truth was she was having last-minute doubts about the wisdom of marrying her fiancé, Jim Blair.

Judging from the anxious look in her mother's eyes as she straightened the wreath of orange blossoms on April's head, April sensed she wasn't the only one to feel uneasy.

Before she had a chance to speak to her mother, there was a commotion outside the dressing room, followed by an urgent knock at the door. A moment later, an obviously agitated usher appeared in the doorway. After apologizing to everyone for his intrusion, he beckoned to the mother of the bride. With a final pat on April's shoulder, Eve Morgan hurried to the door.

A moment later, she hurried back to April's side, a piece of paper in her hand. Her voice was shaking. "Oh, my dear, maybe you should sit down!"

As if one, the five bridesmaids froze.

Rita Rosales dropped her own bouquet and hurried to April's side. Lili Soulé handed the rose-petal-filled flower basket to little Paulette and rushed over, too.

April's heart took a dive. Even before she took the note from her mother's hand, April sensed that something had gone seriously wrong with the wedding.

"What does the note say?" Rita asked, peering over April's shoulder.

April read the note aloud: "'Claire and I have eloped. Jim.'"

"He didn't even say he was sorry," her mother

said. ''Maybe it's all for the best,'' she added slowly as she glanced at the five silent bridesmaids.

Instead of collapsing on the satin-covered bench behind her, April took off her bridal veil and sighed her relief.

Something was finally right.

Chapter One

Six months later

> "A happy relationship requires that a woman make her man feel masculine."
>
> —*The Mating Game*. Lucas Sullivan, Ph.D.

April Morgan, assistant editor of Chicago's *Today's World* magazine, gazed in disbelief at the manuscript in front of her. As an editor of a magazine popular with young professionals, she'd edited a number of strange submissions, but this one beat all.

The article "The Mating Game" was apparently based on a sociological study the author did, originally published in a scientific-community newsletter. The article proposed to enlighten female readers about the behavior men expected in a potential mate. To her growing dismay, the author, an academic, actually went on to list six rules of behavior that he concluded women must follow in order to attract and keep a mate.

From her viewpoint, that of a bride jilted at the altar not too long ago, the article was ludicrous. The author was either naive or deluded. No matter how noteworthy the man's credentials were, assuming they were real, how could any twenty-first-century man actually believe men preferred a Stepford Wife to a real woman?

More to the point, how could any man in his right mind even *want* a woman whose mind had been altered to turn her into a man's idea of an ideal woman?

April frowned. She was aware of other theories that made more sense than his, in particular the one she preferred to believe: a person was driven by a biological imperative to mate with the fittest—read, strong genes—of the opposite gender. To a layperson like her, that clearly meant an innate desire to produce strong and healthy offspring. A goal that she'd been determined to reach before it was too late and that had unwisely led her to the altar.

In retrospect, April realized that accepting Jim's proposal had been prompted by the loud ticking of her biological clock.

But according to this Lucas Sullivan, a man's search for a mate was based solely on a woman's social behavior! Even an academic like him, or perhaps *especially* an academic like him, should have known that choosing a mate was more than merely a game. It was a life-altering choice, one to be made only one time—and very carefully.

She'd learned this the hard way. A wedding fiasco that had left her at the altar at the ripe old age of thirty-two had also left her a lot wiser about men. Most men, she believed, were largely self-centered and chauvinistic like her ex, and as far as she was concerned there wasn't a man currently around her who was worth a second look.

Not that remaining single had been her choice, April mused as she put a question mark in red pencil alongside a sentence she thought needed clarification. If all had gone as she'd planned, she would have honeymooned in Hawaii with that traitorous fiancé of hers, James Elwood Blair. He'd gone on his honeymoon all right, only not with her.

She made additional notations of questions she thought needed answers in the margins of the manuscript and read on. It only became worse.

She had to bite her lip to keep from laughing.

"April, I'm glad to see you're working on 'The Mating Game' article," a familiar voice broke in. "April?"

It took her a moment to realize who was speaking. Ready to apologize for her rudeness, she glanced up at Thomas Eldridge, the magazine's publisher and editor in chief. To her chagrin, he wasn't alone.

"Sorry," she said, gesturing to the manuscript. "I'm afraid I was caught up reading this unbelievable submission. To tell you the truth, I was trying keep from laughing."

"Laughing?" Tom said with a warning frown. He

gestured to the man standing at his side. ''If you think you can contain yourself, I'd like to introduce you to Lucas Sullivan. Lucas and I went to Northwestern together and belonged to the same fraternity. Lucas, this is April Morgan. April is one of our—'' he paused significantly ''—top editors.''

April cringed. Damn. Of all people to have heard her flippant remark, why did it have to be the author of the piece?

Before she could apologize, Tom went on. ''Sullivan here is a noted sociologist, April. The article you have there is one that I asked him to write. The original study was published last year in the National Association of Science Writers newsletter.''

Although her heart was in free fall at her faux pas, April managed to remain calm and look interested.

Tom cleared his throat. ''I should tell you I'm impressed with Lucas's conclusions, which, incidentally, concur with mine.'' He cast April a quelling glance. ''After you get a chance to read the piece again, I'm sure you'll be able to work with him just fine.''

April nodded politely while she digested the subtext of his words—work with him or you're out of a job. She'd been at the magazine long enough to know her still-single boss was a man who took his position as the magazine's publisher and editor in chief very seriously; he wouldn't countenance anyone making light of his decisions.

She couldn't blame him. It was no secret that the

magazine's circulation had been falling steadily in the past six months. Or that Tom had been searching for a way to turn the circulation figures around. But with Sullivan's article? Sure, it was controversial enough, but could such a biased and outdated article accomplish a miracle?

It had to. Her job depended on it.

"I've decided to use Sullivan's article as the lead feature in the September issue," Tom continued, filling her silence. "It'll be a tight squeeze, but we can do it. What do you think, April?"

Speechless, April swung her gaze to Lucas Sullivan. At first glance, the man looked like the stereotypical absentminded professor, a thatch of unruly light brown hair, clothes a little rumpled, smelling ever so slightly of musty old books.

But on second glance... The hairs on the back of her neck began to tingle. Under his staid exterior was one very sexy male. Early thirties, tall and broad-shouldered, he had a nicely sculpted mouth and a chin that begged to be touched. As if that weren't enough, his warm brown eyes were most definitely of the sort called bedroom eyes—heavy lidded and innately sensual. Judging from the hungry stares of the females on the other side of the glass windows of her office, she wasn't the only one to respond to his deceiving appearance. Although to give the man *some* credit, he didn't appear to be aware of it.

"April?" Tom sounded faintly annoyed. "So what do you think?" he repeated.

"Uh..." April considered the question. How could she tell him she had little good to say about the article, its conclusions or, heaven help her, about its author's intelligence when the man was gazing at her expectantly?

If she was honest, she'd admit that her unhappy near miss at matrimony might have colored her opinion of his article. Still, a chauvinist was a chauvinist, no matter what academic credentials he carried. Now, here was a man who, if the rules he espoused in his article were to be believed, had to be the ultimate male chauvinist.

Eldridge frowned. "Something wrong, April?"

"Uh, no," April answered.

She suddenly realized she'd been more than rude.

She rose abruptly and held out her hand. "I'm pleased to meet you, Mr. Sullivan."

He smiled slightly as he took her hand. "Call me Lucas, please," he said with a wary glance at her desk. "Judging by all the red on these pages, you've been bleeding on my manuscript."

Considering the man's stiff body language, April sensed he felt uneasy around her. Not only because she was his editor but because she was a woman. How he'd managed to conduct a sociological study on the subject of male-female relationships if he felt this way was a puzzle.

Tom's disapproval of her editorial opinion or not, she felt it was her job to give Sullivan the truth about his bias before he made a fool of himself and the magazine. She had to manage it diplomatically, of course.

But not just yet. First, she had some thinking to do; she needed to come up with a few ideas of her own to enlighten him.

"I was about to go to lunch, Tom. If you don't mind coming back in an hour or two, Mr. Sull...er, Lucas, I'll be happy to give you my comments."

Tom's scowl of disapproval slowly relaxed, but April sensed she wasn't home free yet. "I was just about to invite Sullivan up to the executive dining room for lunch, April. Oh," he added as he turned to leave, "you can come along if you like."

If she liked? April bit back a tart reply. Although an invitation to the male-dominated executive dining room was considered a coup, it was clear the invitation had been offered as an afterthought. What else could she expect from a man who was not only a personal friend of Sullivan's but actually agreed with his outdated views of women?

"No, thank you, Tom. I've already made plans for lunch." April smiled, went to the door and pointedly waited for him and Sullivan to leave.

To her bemusement, a dozen pairs of female eyes followed Sullivan as he trailed Eldridge to the elevator. With such interest from the opposite sex, it was a puzzle how the man had missed realizing how important it was to have a woman's point of view to help validate his study findings, let alone his ridiculous set of rules.

Once the two men were safely out of sight, April slid Sullivan's article into a folder to share with her close friends Rita Rosales and Lili Soulé at lunch. Rita, a research librarian, and Lili, a graphic artist, both worked at the magazine.

She couldn't wait to show them Sullivan's manuscript. They were sure to share her opinion and appreciate her problem.

Not that Sullivan was her problem unless she made him into one, April reminded herself as she pushed the elevator's down button. As far as she was concerned, her job was only to protect the magazine's outstanding reputation. And herself from being fired. But if she'd known Sullivan before now, he never would have written such a biased study and its resultant article.

Aware of the probable impact on the magazine's readership, it was obviously time for action.

THE BUILDING WHERE THE magazine had its offices was appropriately named the Riverview, since it overlooked the Chicago River. As usual, its popular cafeteria was crowded. Raised voices, the clatter of dishes and the scent of rosemary-fried chicken and garlic mashed potatoes filled the air. A hamburger station, April's target for today, drew her attention.

A double-decker hamburger might not be the healthiest choice of the cafeteria's mouthwatering attractions, but the price was right, April thought as she considered the buffet. She was still in the process of recovering the huge chunk of her savings she'd spent on the wedding dress that still hung in her closet. Despite feeling that the likelihood of her ever needing it was slim, she was strangely reluctant to sell it.

She made her way through the room to where Rita had staked out a corner table. Now was her chance to discuss plans for Sullivan's enlightenment.

Rita smiled wryly as April approached the table. "I can always tell when you have an earthshaking idea on your mind. Something sinful like sex, I hope?"

April dropped her purse and the folder on the table. "Rita Rosales, is sex all you ever think about?"

"Why not?" Rita answered, her green eyes glowing with mischief. "Even if they're not willing to admit it, sex is what everyone thinks about. At least most of the time."

"No, not everyone." April handed Rita the folder that contained Sullivan's manuscript. "Certainly not the author of this article."

Rita's eyes widened in disbelief as she skimmed the first few pages. "You mean a man actually wrote this? How old is he, anyway? Ninety-five?"

"Yes, a man wrote this." April laughed as she searched for her wallet. "In fact, I just met him. His name is Lucas Sullivan and, it turns out, he's an old friend of Tom's. He's a rumpled academic type, the sort who looks like he could have written something like this. But I'd say he's only in his early thirties."

"Get outta here!" Rita pushed her salad aside, opened the folder and proceeded to read out loud. "'While a man is not monogamous by nature, he is more likely to see a woman as a potential girlfriend or mate if sexual intimacy doesn't occur too soon.'"

"I don't believe this," Rita muttered. "Sheesh, look at this—'A woman must strive for compatibility, rather than try to be sexy.'" She flipped to another page. "And what's this crap about a woman 'being generous in her praise of a man's achievements'? This guy seems to think that sexual attraction doesn't count for anything. He's got to be joking."

"Tom doesn't think so. He not only suggested Sullivan write the article, he's making it the lead feature in the September issue."

"What doesn't Tom think?" Lili Soulé, the petite Frenchwoman who completed the trio of friends, arrived at the table slightly out of breath. Perpetually in a rush after trying to keep up with her two lively children, Lili always seemed breathless.

April smiled at her. Lili was a widow and without a man in her life. April believed that her friend had a crush on Tom Eldridge, but was too shy to show it. To make things worse, Tom, along with the rest of the single men on the magazine's staff, hadn't even seemed to notice Lili at last year's company picnic—Lili had been there with her children. Too bad men couldn't see past a ready-made family.

"I'll explain after I get my hamburger," April

said. "Rita, give Lili one of the pages to read until I get back."

Rita was right on, April thought as she made her way to the hamburger station. She considered her friends' obvious physical attractions, Rita's generous curves and Lili's slender beauty. If Sullivan thought that all a woman had to do to be considered a desirable mate was to flatter a man's ego and suppress her sexual urgings, he'd not only never met two women like Rita and Lili, he had a surprise coming. There had to be something lacking in Sullivan's psyche if he actually believed the mating game was played without an initial mutual physical attraction.

Minutes later, April made her way back to the table. "So, what do you think of Sullivan's rules?"

In answer, Lili read aloud: "'A woman must rein in her own desires to promote the health of a relationship.'" She shook her head. "I never would have had the twins if I hadn't shown their father the way I felt about him," she said wistfully. "If this man truly believes this, most women would never have children until they were too old to enjoy them."

Rita patted her hand sympathetically. "At least you have Paul Jr. and Paulette to remember your Paul by." Then abruptly changing gears, she snatched the page from Lili. "Just listen to this one. 'A happy relationship requires that a woman make her man feel masculine.'"

"Without sex? No way," Rita scoffed. "If the man doesn't realize the mating game starts with a sexual attraction he hasn't done his homework. As far as I'm concerned, sex ought to be rule number one."

April laughed and almost choked on her hamburger. "To give the man *some* credit, Rita, I think he only means sexual attraction should be ignored at the *outset* of a relationship."

"No way!" Rita said staunchly. "I still think you have to do something to straighten out this guy's thinking. He's definitely a man who has to be saved from himself."

"Generally speaking, I agree," April said as she took another bite of her hamburger. "I'm sure he has some desirable traits, but—"

"This one is so funny," Lili broke in. She handed the manuscript page back. "'A woman must show her man how much she likes and appreciates him. She must shower him with affection and sublimate her own daily frustrations.'"

"That's supposed to be funny?" Rita said as she took the manuscript page and studied the rule she found offensive. "I don't think so!"

"You're right," Lili agreed with a faint blush. "If I had sublimated my frustrations, I would not have had the twins."

"This one is even nuttier," Rita told her. "'A woman must be supportive, fun loving, easygoing and generous in her praise of a man's achievements.'" She snorted. "Just so long as the guy knows this rule works both ways. Especially the 'supportive' part. You're not really going to let Eldridge print this garbage, are you, April?''

''Not without first suggesting some changes and additions,'' April said, munching on a French fry. ''I don't think he'll like to hear them, but after my narrow escape at the altar, I've come up with a few rules of my own.''

''I'd like to meet this guy to make sure he's real,'' Rita said, reaching for the discarded pickle on April's plate.

''Oh, he's real, all right,'' April said ruefully. ''That's part of the trouble.''

''Only part of the trouble?'' Rita paused in mid bite. ''What's left?''

''Well, you wouldn't know it from his writing—'' April glanced around to make sure she wasn't going to be overheard ''—but Lucas Sullivan is too sexy to be true.''

''Now we're getting somewhere,'' Rita said happily. ''Go on—what does he look like?''

''To start with, golden-brown hair, cleft chin, gorgeous brown eyes.''

Lili stopped eating the peanut-butter-and-jelly sandwich she'd brought from home and stared at April. ''There is more?''

April grinned. ''Isn't that enough?''

Rita sighed into her salad. ''So in spite of his awful views of relationships, you'd still go for him?''

''No. My head is on straighter than that.'' April cleaned up the remains of her lunch, ready to leave.

"I don't intend to fall for a man who thinks the sun sets and rises on the male of the species. Or a man who believes he should be pampered in order to keep him happy." She paused. "I'll just have to come up with a few ideas to straighten him out."

Lili gasped. "But how, April?"

"When Tom comes back from lunch with Sullivan, I'll say I'm going to suggest a few minor revisions. I'm sure Tom will understand."

Rita shrugged. "You're taking a chance. Remember, if Tom contracted the article, he and Sullivan must think alike."

"Probably," April said lightly. "But I think if Sullivan spent more time in the real world, he'd—"

"What is this 'real world'?" Lili interrupted, pulling an apple out of a brown bag and polishing it with a paper napkin before taking a bite.

"The real world where most of us working women live. Not relying just on books or questionnaires," April explained, mentally making notes. "I have a few lessons in mind that should help take care of that. In fact, I can use your help." She stood.

"Not me, April," Lili said. "You're on your own there. Good luck with your Mr. Sullivan."

"Thank goodness he's not mine," April replied. "All I need to do is to try to enlighten the man and move on." She smiled grimly. "See you two later."

UPSTAIRS IN THE BUILDING'S executive dining room, Lucas Sullivan found himself listening with only one ear to Tom Eldridge's praise for his article. A brief nod of his head seemed to be all Tom needed to keep talking. Even Tom's explanation of how he would be paid couldn't keep his attention focused on what Eldridge was saying.

What he *was* focused on was April Morgan. Even though she apparently found his article amusing, which it certainly wasn't meant to be, and was probably the last woman on earth he should be attracted to, he remained fascinated by her flashing eyes and the stubborn tilt of her chin.

He made patterns on the pristine tablecloth with his knife as he half listened to the editor's spiel. The realization he couldn't get April out of his mind actually came as a surprise. It wasn't like him, he mused as he gazed at the menu the waiter handed him and ordered a dessert. Sure, he'd dated a colleague or two, but their conversations had usually been about their respective research projects. Sex had entered the picture now and then, but he'd been too preoccupied with work to form any lasting relationships. Not that he lived like a monk, exactly; he preferred to think of himself as merely discriminating.

With that thought in mind, Lucas mentally measured the auburn-haired Ms. Morgan's attractions on a scale of one to ten. Definitely a ten, he decided as he gazed at his favorite dessert, a chocolate soufflé. Maybe even a ten plus.

"So, what do you think?" Eldridge asked as he

dug into a giant slice of apple pie topped with a generous scoop of vanilla ice cream.

Lucas took a deep swallow of ice water to cool his thoughts. This was, as Eldridge had obviously been trying to tell him for the past forty-five minutes, a business lunch. "About what?"

"April. April Morgan," Eldridge repeated. "How do you feel about working with her?"

Lucas tried to hide his gut reaction to the question; the last thing he wanted to discuss was the way he'd found April not only interesting but infinitely appealing. Or to admit he actually looked forward to getting to know her better on a level other than as an author and his editor.

He frowned. Finding April Morgan attractive was one thing. Having her in a position to criticize and possibly alter his work was another. "Well, since you ask, not much. Don't you have another editor I could work with?"

Eldridge's eyebrows rose in a way that made Lucas uneasy. "No, I'm afraid not. We're shorthanded at the moment, so April will have to do. No criticism of her intended, Sullivan, she's one of the best. April will, of course, check for any grammar and spelling errors, and—if I know her, and I do—she'll try to find a way to make the article a little bit more interesting and exciting. Not all the readers of our magazine are died-in-the-wool academics like yourself."

Lucas's soufflé suddenly tasted like mud. "Change

my article to make it more *exciting?* What's *that* supposed to mean?''

Eldridge took a final swallow of coffee and sat back and smiled. ''I don't know if you intended your work to be controversial, but I believe it is. The rules you espouse for the mating game are bound to create quite a stir in our female readers.''

Warning bells rang in Lucas's mind. ''Stir? What kind of stir?''

Eldridge was beaming. ''Let's just call it a major difference of opinion. The truth is that while I happen to agree with your conclusions about a woman's role in the mating game, I'm willing to bet there are a hell of a lot of women readers who won't. Today's women, especially the type of readers we attract, are sharp, independent and not necessarily interested in marriage. That's the reason I decided to ask you to write the article in the first place. The issue is bound to sell like hotcakes!''

''You're joking!'' Now that he understood the reason behind his former fraternity brother's interest in his study, Lucas felt betrayed.

''Nope, I'm dead serious,'' Eldridge said. ''It'll do miracles for our circulation. You'll drive the women crazy.''

Chapter Two

April managed to run up four flights of stairs to compensate for her lunch time calorie intake before she changed her mind. This type of exercise definitely wasn't for her. She took the elevator the rest of the way.

She should have known Lucas Sullivan would be sitting in her office waiting for her.

Outside of a raised eyebrow and a glance at his watch, he didn't speak. He didn't have to.

She tried a casual smile, slid the folder with his manuscript in it onto her desk, then dropped into her chair. "Sorry to have kept you waiting."

He shot a telling glance at the pages that had slid out from the protective folder. "Did you enjoy your fries?"

Of all the things she'd expected him to say, a question about her lunch wasn't it. "How did you know I had fries for lunch?"

"Easy." He leaned across the desk and pointed to the top page of his manuscript.

April followed his finger to where a liberal blot of ketchup rested on one of his rules. "A happy relationship requires that a woman make her man feel masculine."

To her private satisfaction, the ketchup stain almost obliterated what she considered to be one of his more offensive rules. A man who didn't feel secure in his own masculinity wasn't going to get her sympathy.

She decided to try a little humor. "It's an editorial comment." She reached for a tissue and tried to blot the stain away, but all she managed to accomplish was to create a wider smudge on the page, which made the rule completely illegible. "Well, actually, it's a deletion!"

She laughed and looked up at Sullivan. He didn't seem the in the least amused. "I can get a clean page to work with," she said. "Give me a moment." She picked up the phone, punched a number and spoke into the receiver rapidly, then hung up. "I've asked for another copy of page one."

April tossed the stained tissue into a wastepaper basket under her desk and waited for Sullivan to explode. But outside of a raised eyebrow, he didn't look upset. Instead, he looked watchful, grim.

She wouldn't be surprised if Tom had assured him the article would be published as is. He'd said he agreed with Sullivan's conclusions, after all.

She made a show of rifling through the rest of the manuscript pages. "I'm just about finished making a few suggestions in the margins I think would be helpful.''

Sullivan's eyebrows knit a frown. ''Such as?'' he asked quietly, but she could see, from the pulse throbbing in his temple and the rigidity of his body, what the effort to keep from losing his cool cost him.

April smothered a sigh. She knew enough about the academic world to understand that a professor's reputation depended on continuing to publish. After all, she had to concede, while journalism was her game, he was a noted social scientist. She should have known he wasn't prepared to take her advice lightly.

In an attempt to soothe Sullivan's ruffled feathers, she smiled soothingly and moved on. ''I've never edited a submission that couldn't use a *few* changes, if only to make it more appealing to our readers. I'm very aware of who our readers are, their likes and dislikes.''

''In the case of your article,'' she continued when he didn't comment, ''I think we need to make a few revisions, in tone if not content. Left as is, I'm afraid the piece is bound to cause a riot among female readers.''

''Strange,'' he said thoughtfully. ''That's what Tom said at lunch. ''But he sounded as if it was a *positive* thing, not negative. But I still say no to any changes. I take every word I write seriously.''

''Of course, Mr.…er Lucas,'' April agreed. ''As your editor, I feel it's my job to suggest constructive changes without altering your original thesis—if for no other reason than to keep your reader's attention."

"I don't think you understand," he said. "My original study was published in a scientific journal. Tom asked me to write this article based on that study."

"I know, but—"

"No buts. My conclusions aren't just a matter of my own opinions. I interviewed a number of grad students and volunteers before I drew those conclusions."

"I didn't mean to insult you," April said, trying for some kind of common meeting ground. "The subject of your article *is* quite controversial. I'm sure you're aware of a couple of alternative theories about the mating game that are more acceptable to women." *Including to her.*

"Of course, the survival of the fittest," he agreed. "The selfish-gene theory. Frankly, I don't think many people stop to think about finding a mate with strong genes to pass on to their offspring."

April shifted uneasily. "There is another theory, you know."

"You're no doubt referring to sexual attraction," he said with a shrug. "That, however, is merely a matter of biology."

April could hear Rita's derisive laughter.

Mesmerized by his disparaging assessment of what surely had to be an important aspect of the mating game, April managed to nod. "Still, a lot of people believe it to be true."

His gaze changed suddenly. Became warm, roved over her facial features and came to rest on her lips. She almost squirmed.

"I'm a scientist, or if you prefer, a social scientist, Ms. Morgan. My work is based on an actual sociological study of relationships." His gaze now moved down to her throat. "If you question my credentials, I would be more than happy to provide them for you."

April raised a hand to make sure the buttons on her blouse were securely fastened. If Sullivan only knew, his *credentials* weren't in question. Not his physical ones, anyway, she thought guiltily as her gaze roamed over his seated frame. How could he not know that those eyes of his could turn a marble statue into a pile of dust?

Rita had been more on target about sex than she knew. What April had hoped would be a constructive exchange of ideas suddenly seemed to have turned into a frank appraisal of a mutual sexual attraction. If Sullivan thought sex was a natural magnet between the male and female species, how in heaven's name had he come up with a set of rules no woman in her right mind would buy into?

"It's not your credentials I question," she finally said. "It's your conclusions."

This time his eyebrows arched almost to his hairline, and the pulse in his temple increased.

Not a good omen for a compromise, April figured. Not when he managed to continue to look sexy as hell, in spite of his anger. She had to remind herself she was the man's editor and not a potential playmate. That she wasn't offering herself as a candidate for the mating game.

She felt compelled to add, "I can't bring myself to believe you were serious when you wrote these rules, Mr. Sullivan—Lucas."

This got his undivided attention. "Serious? Damn right I was serious. Still am! What I was trying to say is that sexual attraction should be resisted. At least initially."

April took heart. What was becoming clear was that Sullivan had seldom been questioned, let alone told by anyone that his work was a subject for laughter. She wasn't sorry she'd been the one to do it. She might have been a little too frank, but at least he was paying attention.

"Okay, let's talk about your interpretation of your research," April said.

Sullivan still looked annoyed, but he shrugged. "Go ahead. Talk."

"Well," she began, "I'm afraid your interpretation is biased. How many people did you interview during the course of your original study?"

He squared his jaw. "The figures are in the original study, but there were 176."

"And that included both men and women, right?"

"Naturally," he replied. "How else could this have been an empirical study?"

"Of course," April agreed. Privately, she had a strong feeling the final ratio of male to female volunteers had either been skewed in favor of males or he'd been subconsciously biased in his interpretations of the answers to his questions.

"How much did you pay the volunteers? The going rate of seven dollars an hour?"

"No." He sat back, obviously pleased with himself. "Actually I was very generous. I paid ten."

April sighed. "When I was a journalism major at Northwestern, for ten dollars an hour, I would have told you anything I thought you wanted to hear."

His eyes narrowed. "What's that supposed to mean?"

"Simply that the subjects you queried were perhaps not being truthful."

Lucas leaned across the desk, eye to eye, nose to nose, so closely she could feel the heat of his skin. "No way! My conclusions are based on actual replies to my questions."

"Sure, and only because of the way you *formed* the questions," April said. "Pardon me for saying so, but I don't think your study was unbiased. Therefore, any article based on your original study has also to be biased. I'm just saying that we need to take a closer look at your conclusions."

Lucas felt his temper rise, a luxury he seldom allowed himself, let alone in a professional setting. Not only at April's opinion of his research methods, but at himself for allowing his attraction to her to influence his professional approach to the subject of the mating game. "You think so, do you?"

"Yes, I do. My job as your editor is to make constructive suggestions."

"That may be your usual job," he said, distracted by the way April's eyes seemed to change from brown to shades of green flecked with gold. "But it doesn't apply here. I repeat—not when the work in question is based on a scientific study."

"Maybe," April said, "although there's science and there's *science*. However, you should be aware that if your article appears in its present form, it's bound to cause a great deal of controversy. The kind of feedback you might not like to hear."

Determined to overlook April's challenge to his professionalism, Lucas took a deep breath. "I still stand by my work."

"Even if I can persuade you otherwise?"

"Careful, Ms. Morgan." A calculating smile came over his face. "You're treading on thin ice. What would you do if I took you up on your offer?"

April wondered if he actually realized he'd made a sexual innuendo. If so, there had to be more to Sullivan than met the eye. She cleared her throat. "Perhaps we should leave this discussion for tomorrow? It'll give me time to go over your article more carefully."

"Yes, of course." He rose to his feet. "Not too early, please. I'm going to be up late tonight."

"Research?"

"In a manner of speaking," he said as he turned to leave.

April wondered about the glint in his eye.

"By the way," she said as she made a show of straightening the manuscript pages, "how was your lunch in the executive dining room?"

Lucas turned back. "Okay. What makes you ask?"

"Just okay?" April reached into her purse for a tissue. "Not if you had their chocolate soufflé for dessert."

"How did you know?"

Ignoring the urge to wipe the bit of chocolate off his chin, April handed Lucas the tissue. "You have some chocolate on the corner of your chin. If there's anything I recognize, it's chocolate soufflé. It happens to be a favorite of mine."

Lucas rubbed at his chin with the tissue and, to her surprise, winked. "I'll have to remember that important detail—and a few other things, as well."

April wondered what he meant by "a few other things." She only knew that the phrase and the way he delivered it caused butterflies to flutter through her midsection.

"I'll call you later this afternoon to make an appointment," she said.

"Sorry," Sullivan said, "but I won't be home to

take the call. Let's just say I'll try to be here as early as I can tomorrow morning and leave it at that, all right?''

He would *try?* Most academics would give a year's salary to be published in *Today's World*, an eclectic magazine with far more readers than any scientific journal. ''What can be more important than our discussing your article?''

''I play in a small band. We're practicing this afternoon for a performance tonight.''

''A chamber music quartet?''

''Uh, not exactly.''

The reluctance in Sullivan's voice whetted April's curiosity. ''How, 'not exactly'?''

''Actually, it's a rock band and I play lead guitar.''

April didn't believe him, but she didn't let on. ''Uh, where did you say you were performing tonight?''

''I didn't, but we'll be at the Roxy on the north side of town. Why?''

''Just curious.'' It wasn't easy for April to keep a straight face when laughter at the absurdity of a serious academic playing in a rock band threatened to overcome her, but she managed. She'd already laughed at one of the man's endeavors; to laugh at another might totally alienate Sullivan, not to mention cost her her job.

There must have been something in her voice that made him turn back at the door. ''You don't believe me?''

"I do. It's just such a surprise," she said quickly. "You not only teach, you write. How in heaven's name do you manage to find time to be in a rock band?"

"Call it an instinct for survival," he said, gazing at her as if his mind were a hundred miles away. "Actually, being raised by a strict father to become a successful academic, then getting my advanced degree so I could do research and teach, hasn't left me a lot of time to pursue music, but music, in particular rock music, is my passion. It's the one thing I do that satisfies my soul, and I find I must make time for it."

Fascinated by the little speech and what it revealed about the man, April tried to imagine the dry and factual world Sullivan had grown up in. Her heart wept at the thought of a child's yearning for the freedom to express himself that had had to wait until he was a grown man.

"You must hate your father," she said softly.

"No, not at all," he replied. "And as I get older, I think I actually understand him better. The divorce from my mother damn near bankrupted him financially. And then her accidental death shortly after they reconciled bankrupted him emotionally."

April made a sound of sympathy.

"The only way Dad said he could be sure I would never lose everything I had," Sullivan continued, "was to see to it I concentrated on my education and to keep women on a back burner." He shrugged. "I haven't been exactly overjoyed at the way I live, but I can't fault him for that. He meant well.''

April thought of her own childhood. She and her two older brothers had been very competitive, each trying to outdo the other in everything—school, sports and parental attention. Her growing-up years hadn't been all fun and games, but at least she'd had two loving parents.

''And so now you have your band,'' she said softly.

His face brightened. ''Yeah. I picked up guitar several years back from a friend of mine. Turns out I'm pretty decent at the guitar. It was just a matter of time before two of my friends taught me the ropes and we formed a band. We trade off. They write the music, I write the lyrics. We try to practice a couple of times a week and perform about twice a month. I don't mind saying we're pretty good.''

''And you're playing tonight.''

''Yes, but don't worry, I'll be ready for you tomorrow morning.''

Unable to explain her reaction to Sullivan's unexpected fall from the lofty academic perch on which she'd placed him, April waved him off. ''It doesn't really matter. Go on, have fun. I'll see you here tomorrow.''

April followed Lucas to her office door and stood watching the envious glances that followed him to the elevator. Maybe she shouldn't have been so surprised at his choice for recreational activities. For a man so serious, so preoccupied with sociological research, performing in a rock band had to be a harmless way of releasing emotions.

She turned back to her desk and tried to concentrate on Sullivan's article. It would have been a lot easier to be objective if the author's warm brown eyes, his innate masculine charm and his story about his childhood didn't keep getting in the way.

Sullivan really did need to be introduced to a woman's real world for more reasons than one, she mused as she scowled at an offensive phrase in the manuscript. Still, becoming too emotionally involved with him wasn't a good idea. Not only as his editor, but as a woman. She'd have to rethink their relationship.

But not before she paid a visit to the Roxy.

"COOL!" RITA SQUEALED when April called and invited her to go with her to the Roxy to hear Sullivan play. "Are you talking about the same guy who wrote that mating game article?"

"Bingo." April smiled at Rita's surprised reaction. After reading his article, the idea of Lucas Sullivan playing his heart out with a guitar surprised her, too.

"I'm all yours." Rita's eager voice came over the phone. "What time?"

"I'll pick you up around eight." April laughed as she hung up the phone. She could visualize her hip friend reaching for her lipstick—a bloodred hue to match the hot blood that ran in her veins.

Not that April was fooled. She knew that Rita's frank talk was meant to shock, and that she, like herself and Lili, was waiting for the right man to come along.

Again April tried, without success, to concentrate on Sullivan's article. She had a growing suspicion she'd been wrong about him. There were his brief flashes of sexy innuendos, the occasional glint in his eye, and now, his music. Rock, no less!

She sighed as she put a question mark alongside one of his rules. Why was she wasting time trying to figure out this man?

A secret visit to the Roxy was definitely in order.

OVER RITA'S OBJECTIONS, April led the way past the sign on the door that announced the Rocking Eagles were appearing that night. She claimed a small table in the far corner. The room was dark, except for the flashes of color coming from roaming klieg lights. A billboard by the door announced Sullivan's band—suddenly the other patrons began to cheer and called for the band to begin.

The stage darkened. The slow, sensuous beat of a drum sounded. A bass guitar joined in, then a keyboard. An unseen voice began to sing. Pandemonium broke out. The small dance floor in front of the bandstand became a sea of swaying bodies.

"Where's Sullivan?" Rita shouted above the noise.

April's eyes were riveted to the stage. "I don't see him. Maybe this isn't his band, after all."

April climbed onto her chair to get a better look at the musicians on the stage. The drummer wore black slacks and a black T-shirt. A red bandanna held back his long hair. The bass player wore black jeans and a red T-shirt with Rocking Eagles emblazoned across the front. The keyboard player was also in red and black, clearly the band's colors.

But where was Sullivan?

Suddenly the drummer beat a sort of drumroll, and another band member, this one in black leather pants and an open black shirt and wielding a red guitar, leaped onto the stage. He grabbed the microphone and began to sing a song about the train being late at the station. Dazed, April took the words to mean that he'd been too late to tell his girl he loved her in time to claim her for his own.

She took a closer look. *Sullivan?*

April climbed down from her chair and sat. Either the man was Sullivan's identical twin or she'd been had. How else could the man have come up with an article like his with a straight face?

"What a hottie!" Rita exclaimed admiringly. "If that's the guy you were talking about, April, you've got yourself a real man!"

April's head swam. "Save your breath, the man's

not mine. After tonight, I'm not even sure what I'd do with him if he were!''

She grabbed Rita by the wrist. ''I've got to get out of here before the lights come on and Sullivan sees me.''

Rita hung back. ''We just got here! I'm having a great time!''

''I'm not, and we're leaving,'' April said with a nervous glance at the stage. Sullivan had turned his back on the audience and was sliding sensually across the stage, his leather-clad behind eliciting cheers from female fans. She gulped. ''Hurry! I'll make it up to you, I swear. I'll even take you out for a hamburger on the way home.''

''A hamburger isn't going to make up for missing Sullivan move that tush of his,'' Rita said with a longing look at the stage. ''Who would have thought it?''

''Not me,'' April said as she realized she would never be able to look Lucas straight in the eyes again without seeing his swaying hips and naked chest.

Chapter Three

The next morning, April made a point to be in her office early. A rock musician might be unpredictable, but the man who wrote "The Mating Game" was bound to be on time.

As she settled down at her desk, she thought about the rule "A woman must strive for compatibility, rather than try to be sexy."

Compatibility was okay with her, she told herself. The sexy part was definitely out.

Until she glanced down at her new sea-green linen suit and the form-fitting silk blouse. Then there was her perfume, a scent that had cost her a bundle and she almost never wore. The glimpse of Sullivan performing on stage last night must have muddled her thinking. Why else would she have gone to such lengths to look so feminine today? So sexy.

Was it because she believed in the popular scientific theory that the basis for the mating game was a search for someone with the right stuff? And that she'd found it in Sullivan?

Was it because, in defiance of his conclusions in his article, she was out to show him the attraction between the sexes was more important than rational thinking?

Or because Sullivan's sexuality had gotten to her?

Impossible!

To her dismay, Sullivan found her in the midst of her mental debate.

"Good morning," he said cheerfully.

"Good morning." April caught herself before something about his performance last night escaped her lips. She didn't want him to know she'd been there. "How was last night?"

"Great!" He yawned before he sat down. "Sorry, I was up late. Couldn't sleep. How about you?"

"I slept like a baby, thank you." The truth was, she hadn't slept much last night, either. "So I took a closer look at the article, and as I was saying yesterday..." Her voice trailed off. How could she focus on business when the vision of a pair of perfect buns encased in black leather kept getting in the way?

She studied Sullivan. His eyes were half closed. He didn't appear any more interested in the business at hand than she was. "Lucas?"

He took a deep breath and sat up straighter. "Yes?"

"You're not paying attention to what I'm saying."

"Sorry. I'm afraid I'm a little groggy after last night." Lucas knew the lack of sleep wasn't the only thing wrong with him today. It was April Morgan's scent, her enchanting feminine appearance.

The lush auburn hair that fell softly around her face and the lips that begged to be kissed.

He forced himself to focus on business. "I was hoping you've reconsidered asking me to make changes."

"No, actually there are still a few. That is, if you want me to take your article seriously." She settled her glasses on her nose and picked up a red pencil. "Perhaps—"

Before she could go on, a young woman with a glint in her eye came into the office. "Is there anything I can do for you, April?"

April smothered a groan. Judging from the avid interest in the intruder's wide blue eyes as she gazed at Sullivan, an introduction was expected.

"Lucas, this is Tiffany Waters. She's our college intern and works for us in the summers. Tiffany, this is Lucas Sullivan. We were discussing an article Mr. Sullivan submitted for publication."

Sullivan stood politely. "Nice to meet you, Ms. Waters."

"Nice to meet you, too," a breathless Tiffany said as she held out her hand for Sullivan to take. She gazed soulfully into his eyes. "Really, really nice."

Obviously Tiffany, too, had managed to see beneath the man's academic exterior. A man who not only was the target of a blatant sexual invitation but was returning it, if April were to judge by the way he held Tiffany's hand a little too long and returned her gaze.

Was this the same man who, only yesterday, had appeared uncomfortable around women? Or had she been the only woman he was uncomfortable with?

"Thank you, Tiffany, but we have everything we need." April escorted the mesmerized intern to the door. "Before you try to seduce the man," she told her under her breath, "let me tell you that Mr. Sullivan is an academic more accustomed to books than people. Even if you were able to lure him into bed, I'm not sure he would know what to do with you."

Doubtful, Tiffany glanced back over her shoulder. "You think, April? Gee, what a waste of good material!"

"I think," April said as she moved Tiffany closer to the door. "Trust me, he's definitely not the type a vibrant young woman like yourself should become involved with."

With April occupied persuading a reluctant Tiffany to move on, Lucas turned away to look out the window at the clusters of cumulus clouds floating across Chicago's skyline. April had a lot to learn about him, namely that there was nothing wrong with his hearing, nor with his manhood and skills in the bedroom.

He wouldn't know what to do with a woman like Tiffany? When hell froze over!

As for April, if he read the sparks in her eyes correctly, and he was damn sure he did, there was a banked fire burning inside her waiting to be ignited. Why a man hadn't already staked out his territory was a puzzle. It just wasn't going to be him.

Too bad, he mused as he watched April at the door with Tiffany. April might not know it, but she was all woman, the type who got under a man's skin faster than the Tiffanys of the world.

She was tall enough to fit comfortably under his chin, he mused as he made an inventory of her shapely figure. Just the right size to cradle in his arms and to explore her chameleon eyes. Even if she didn't fit the description of what made women desirable in his article, he was attracted to her.

After all, his article merely recapped his thesis that sexual attraction wasn't of primary importance. His underlying thesis was that the domestic and companionship qualities of a relationship were. Was it his fault that his conclusions were being interpreted as a series of rules for a woman to get her man?

That brought him back to April.

Lucas sighed as his thoughts drifted down sensual paths he'd been too busy to visit before he'd met April. It seemed he wasn't that busy now.

"Are you with me, Lucas?"

April's question caught his attention. With her? Definitely, for all the good it would do him. "Sorry, why don't you run whatever it was you said by me one more time?"

She was back at her desk, peering over her reading glasses. "I said it might be a good idea to rename your article in order to catch the attention of our readers. What do you think of calling it 'Sullivan's Rules'?"

Lucas thought for a moment. "Okay," he agreed reluctantly, "but please remember these aren't really rules. What you see there are conclusions based on an empirical study."

"So you've said," April agreed with a tight smile. "Anything else?" Lucas idly wondered if April was aware of how attractive she looked with her reading glasses slipping lower on her adorable nose. Or if she realized how charming she looked when her single dimple betrayed her inner thoughts by dancing across her right cheek?

Was she laughing at him again?

"Frankly," April continued, "I do have a few other minor comments."

Lucas caught himself admiring the graceful curve of her neck. "Okay. Say, how about I call you April, instead of Ms. Morgan?"

Taken by surprise, April took off her glasses and rubbed the bridge of her nose. "If it will make you feel more comfortable." She pointed to a paragraph and read aloud. "'A woman must rein in her own desires to promote the health of a relationship.'" She paused for effect. "Sounds like Victorian thinking, don't you agree?"

"For today's marriage, yes," Lucas agreed. "For companionship, no. A number of my friends have live-in companions and seem happy enough. However, I've found that most men still prefer to take the lead in a permanent relationship.''

''Before or after the woman tries to make her man feel masculine? Or before she makes an effort not to influence him by being sexy?''

''Well, when you put it that way...'' He tried not to dwell on the way the color of her eyes deepened when she was disturbed.

''Exactly,'' she agreed, and put her glasses back on. ''Let's move on. How about women showering their men with affection? Shouldn't that be left out, too? Or haven't you considered that the close physical proximity that showering affection might entail would break your rules for a premarital relationship?''

''Not if the parties set the ground rules before they enter the relationship.'' Lucas tried to ignore an inner warning voice reminding him he was letting his testosterone get in the way of rational thinking. ''Intelligent people shouldn't allow their bodies to rule their minds.''

April smothered a comment. If he actually believed that garbage, where was the man in the black leather pants? The *tight* black leather pants. ''Mind over matter—right. An interesting theory, but you seem to have forgotten the most important factors in the search for a lasting relationship.''

Lucas shifted uneasily in his chair and glanced at the door. Things were getting a little too warm for comfort. He would have given a bundle for another interruption. "And what factors are they?"

"There's that popular scientific theory about the subconscious instinctive desire to find a mate with strong genes."

"Of course." Lucas shrugged. "However, it was my intention to show the sociological aspect of the mating game, not to dwell on what amounts to little more than what I call *biolust.*"

Biolust! April bit her lower lip to keep from bursting into laughter. "Interesting theory. So tell me—how have your rules worked for you?"

"*I* wasn't looking for a mate," he answered. "I was merely making important sociological observations."

"While we're at it," April continued with a hopeless glance at his article, "how about love? Or isn't falling in love supposed to enter the picture?"

Lucas thought of haunting memories of his warring parents, their sorry relationship, a divorce, remarriage and the subsequent death of his mother.

"Love is a transitory emotion and can be controlled," he said. "Especially since it's what gets in the way of an intelligent choice for a marital partner. At best, love only exists in novels and movies."

Lucas paused to admire the fascinating golden sparks in April's eyes.

"Lucas? You've gone somewhere else again!"

"Sorry," he said. "Look, you're quarreling over a serious study, April. Tom didn't seem to think I was off base when he called me and asked me to write the article you have there.''

''That's because he's a man.'' *Or a true chauvinist like Sullivan himself.* ''However, since our magazine has more female than male readers, I honestly think you should try to lighten it up before it gets published.''

He looked incredulous. ''The article was drawn from an empirical study. How the hell can it be lightened up?''

''Well, maybe you need to use a tongue-in-cheek approach. Or if you don't like that, maybe a few female opinions are needed to sway you.''

Lucas straightened. ''Are you're going to offer me yours?''

The flame in April's eyes grew brighter. ''Are you asking?''

''Sure,'' Lucas said, confident that April wouldn't be able to come up with any valid reasons to change his article. Hell, if he began to doubt his research methods or his conclusions, he might as well admit to doubting himself. ''I'm game. Go ahead.''

As far as he was concerned, the gauntlet had been thrown down and he was man enough to pick it up. Between Tom Eldridge's remark about setting the magazine's readership on fire with the article and April's challenge to lighten it up, he could hardly sit by and just become an amusing topic of dinner conversation.

April considered giving him the whole nine yards

of her opinion. If only the mental picture of the man as he'd appeared last night on stage didn't keep getting in the way.

On the other hand, the idea of giving Sullivan a few lessons on what went on in the real world, instead of in books, became more enticing by the minute.

Of course, educating him wasn't going to be easy. Like most of the men she'd already dubbed a "Sullivan," he seemed to have the ability to compartmentalize the various areas of his life. As far as she was concerned, it was nothing more than tunnel vision.

She took off her glasses again. "To tell you the truth, I've decided not to waste time telling you what I think. I intend to take you out and *show* you. Humanize you a little."

"I'm all yours," he replied casually. "When do we begin?"

"Hot coffee, tea or..." To April's dismay, the young office gofer, Arthur Putnam, cheerfully rolled a refreshment cart to the office door.

"Not now, Arthur, but thanks for the offer," April said with a careful eye on Lucas. "We're really busy here."

Lucas held up his hand. "Just a minute, please. I don't know about you, April, but after last night I could use a cup of strong, black coffee."

Arthur's eyes lit up at the mention of last night. "It's not what you're thinking, Arthur," April said hastily. "Mr. Sullivan performed in a rock and roll band last night."

Arthur closed his mouth. After a dubious glance at Lucas, he shrugged. "If you say so."

Lucas reached into his jacket pocket, extracted a card and wrote on the back of it. "Drop in anytime—as my guest."

Arthur's face lit up. "Gee, thanks!"

April gave up trying to keep Sullivan's mind on business, but she wasn't through with him yet. As for Arthur's visit, she would have been annoyed if she hadn't known that Arthur was in the throes of puppy love, with *her* of all people, and had only been momentarily distracted.

At least Arthur wasn't another Tiffany hitting on Lucas, April thought wryly. Judging from the number of women who'd found a need to pass by her office this morning, word about Sullivan's presence had spread like wildfire.

Unfortunately, the morning was still young.

Resigned to the inevitable, at least for now, April beckoned to Arthur. She couldn't bring herself to be upset with him. Not when he was one of the few men around the office who wasn't impressed with his maleness.

"Come on in, Arthur. By the way, Lucas, this angel of mercy is Arthur Putnam. Arthur, this is Lucas Sullivan—he's the author of an article we're going to publish."

Arthur was too busy gazing adoringly at April to reply.

"Arthur! Mr. Sullivan asked for a cup of black coffee."

"Sorry." Unabashed, a grinning Arthur tore his gaze away. He poured a cup of coffee and handed it over. "What's the subject of your article?"

"I call it 'The Mating Game.' It's not what you think," Lucas added hurriedly when Arthur's eyes widened. "It's based on an earlier publication of mine, a sociological study about what men want in a wife."

Arthur turned his adoring gaze back to April, his meaning clear. She was his idea of the ideal woman. "Anything for you, Ms. Morgan?"

"No, thank you. Perhaps later."

"Sure. I'll be back. You can bet on it." With a last soulful look at April, Arthur rolled the beverage cart out the door.

Lucas smothered a grin. Apparently, he wasn't the only one who'd noticed April's striking appearance today.

Maybe it wasn't too late to revise his article to include something about how a woman should dress in order to please the man she was interested in?

He looked at April. "You were saying before we were interrupted?"

"That there's a great deal more to the attraction between the sexes than what you describe in your article, and I'm going to take you out and show you,'' April said as she gathered her purse and portfolio. ''Shall we go?''

When, Lucas thought, had the question of protecting his research methods turned into something to do with April?

After admitting to himself he found her attractive? After her offer to humanize him?

''Why not?'' He set his half-empty cup on the desk and made a show of looking eager to learn about the real world. ''I can hardly wait.''

''April, are you busy?'' A lush brunette paused at the office door, leaned against the frame and frankly studied Lucas.

April swallowed a groan. After last night, she might have known Rita would show up today to get a closer look at Sullivan. She beckoned her friend into the office. ''Hi, Rita. I am busy, but not as busy as we expect to be soon,'' she added meaningfully.

Rita's eyes lit up as she misinterpreted April's answer. ''Get outta here!''

April swallowed hard. ''As long as you're here, you might as well come in and meet Lucas Sullivan. Mr. Sullivan is the author of the article I told you about yesterday. Lucas, I'd like you to meet Rita Rosales. Rita is our research librarian.''

Undeterred by April's hint to make her visit short, Rita sashayed into the office. ''I'm pleased to meet you, Mr. Sullivan. Although, to be honest, I can't say I agree with your article. I'd say that there's a lot more important going on between the sexes than just a woman feeding a man's ego.''

Lucas wasn't surprised at the mini critique. Any friend of April's was bound to disagree with him. As for Rita, she fit right in at this admittedly eclectic publication.

''I'm not surprised to hear that,'' he answered wryly. ''Just as I won't be surprised to learn you're about to enlighten me.''

''Rita, don't you dare!'' April broke in before Rita could launch into her theory that the basis for male-female relationships was purely sexual attraction. Or, as Rita often said in plain terms, good old-fashioned sex.

Undeterred, Rita grinned at Lucas. ''You sure don't look like the man who came up with that old-fashioned set of rules April showed me.''

'''The Mating Game' article is not just a set of rules,'' Lucas corrected her automatically before he realized he'd just been given a compliment. ''I'm not?''

''No. I figured you would either be elderly or a stuffed shirt. As for being old, you're obviously not. As for stuffy...'' Her voice trailed off as her gaze swept Lucas. ''You've sure got what it takes to get a gal's attention. Maybe there's hope for you yet.'' She winked at April. ''Don't give up, April. With a little work, I think you can wake up your Mr. Sullivan.''

Rita's unsolicited assessment of Sullivan's attractions might be embarrassing, but it was dead on. April grabbed Rita by the arm and urged her to the door before her friend mentioned her visit to the Roxy. "The next time you have something important to tell me, please use the telephone." Under her breath, she added, "I'll be up to see you later."

"Sure, now that I've met your Mr. Sullivan, I think it can wait. Just remember what I told you." Rita grinned at him over her shoulder. "See you later."

Lucas settled back into his chair. At the rate they'd been interrupted, there wouldn't be enough hours left in the day for April to take him out and try to humanize him. "Interesting woman," he commented. "I wouldn't mind hearing her explain her version of how a man chooses the woman he'd like to spend the rest of his life with."

"You don't want to know," April said, unable to imagine Rita's raw sex talk without laughing. She pushed a few errant strands of hair away from her eyes. "Rita tends to be frank, but I assure you that it's all talk. As for what she actually thinks on the subject, I'm not sure you'd want to hear that, either."

Lucas smiled. "Why not? I heard the birds-and-bees talk when I was ten. I've even managed to teach a few classes on marriage and the family without blushing."

"I wish it were that simple," April muttered as heat rose to her throat. "I don't know about you, but I'm afraid I'm not up to an X-rated conversation."

A roguish grin spread over Lucas's face. His brown eyes turned a deeper brown. ''Try me.''

Mutely, April stared at the man whom only twenty-four hours ago she'd labeled as a stuffy academic. Now that she'd glimpsed the other side of him, she was afraid that the last thing she would be able to manage was a frank discussion of sexual attraction.

Something was definitely wrong here.

The heat continued its upward journey into her cheeks. ''It's not exactly a professional topic for us to discuss. I'm your editor, not your biology teacher.''

''Too bad.'' Lucas formed his features into an exaggerated display of regret. ''You would have been great.''

April managed a weak smile.

''So,'' he said next, ''unless you're expecting more visitors, shall we get on with this show of yours before someone else drops in?''

As he spoke, there was gentle knock at the door.

''April? I'm sorry to interrupt you when you're busy, but you left a page of the manuscript in the cafeteria.''

Lili? Lili, the friend who had declined to become involved in humanizing Lucas Sullivan yet couldn't resist meeting him?

April glanced at the printed page Lili offered. A quick glance told her that Sullivan's fame had spread so throughout the building that even the prim-and-proper Lili couldn't ignore it.

Resigned to the inevitable, April made the introductions. "Lili works in the art department as a graphic artist, Lucas. She's also a very good friend of mine. Please try to remember that we all try to be professional around here."

With a wry smile, Lucas rose to his feet. "Of course. Happy to meet you, Ms. Soulé."

"I am happy to meet you, too." She handed April the sheet of paper and backed to the door. "I will see you later, April."

After Lili blushed her way out of the office, Lucas chuckled. "Maybe we should put off our excursion. I wouldn't want to disappoint the rest of your friends."

April was really annoyed. Any notion that she may have misjudged Lucas vanished. The man was a prime example of a chauvinistic male with an ego to match. "I swear I had nothing to do with those visits. It has to be all your fault."

"My fault?" Lucas looked affronted. "All I did was to show up here this morning. At your request, I might add."

How could one man have such an innate male appeal and still wind up the author of such naive conclusions about relationships? April wondered. All the man seemed to know about women would fit into a thimble.

She was tempted to find Tom and tell him about Sullivan's appearance at the Roxy, just to prove that Lucas Sullivan wasn't the man he appeared to be.

But then, if they'd attended Northwestern together, maybe Tom already knew the truth about Sullivan.

Nothing was going to keep the magazine article from creating a riot among its female readers, April was certain. The bigger problem, once the magazine hit the stands, was how to protect Sullivan from himself.

Chapter Four

Curious about April and the world she lived in, Lucas wandered around her office. Framed magazine covers hung on the walls. A plaque testifying that the magazine had taken honors in the field of journalism for the past three years occupied a prominent place. An award for the outstanding employee of the month bore April's name.

Neat, small stacks of manuscripts waiting to be read covered a corner of April's desk. A computer, monitor and a handy cup of black and red pencils the other.

To the casual eye, April might appear to be all business. To his trained senses, he knew she was more complex than that. Underneath her professional demeanor lurked a passionate woman, he was sure. He'd give a lot to see that passion.

He dug his hands into his pockets and paused to gaze down at the Chicago River and a passing cruise boat. He'd always taken the river for granted. Today, the river had possibilities. The idea of cruising through downtown Chicago with April, who wanted to show him a different world while he got to know her better, sounded interesting.

He wasn't going to wait for April to think of the cruise as a setting for his enlightenment; he'd do the inviting himself.

He wandered over to April's desk, glanced into the open middle drawer and grimaced. The top page of his manuscript was covered with brief notations in the margins.

He turned away. April had a right to her own opinions about the mating game—as long as she didn't expect him to change his.

Aware of April's interest in him, as well as his unexpected interest in her, there was only one thing left for him to do. He had to get April out of the office where they wouldn't be disturbed.

He hadn't spent his adult years in the study of relationships to be swayed by a pair of hazel eyes.

"Busy office you have here," Lucas said when April walked back into her office. He wasn't sure what she'd meant by "freshening up," but in that eye-riveting outfit and shoes with heels that made her legs go on forever, she looked awfully good to him.

"Not usually," April replied as she noticed the direction of his gaze. She tugged at her skirt, as if by doing so, she could make it longer. She couldn't. "Apparently, word about you has gotten around the company. I suppose it was bound to happen."

Lucas dragged his eyes from her legs. ''The article was taken from an empirical study!''

''So you keep saying.'' As if expecting further visitors, April glanced at the door.

Sullivan took the next—and to him, logical—step. ''Since it looks as if we're not going to have any privacy around here, how about if we take time off for a river cruise?''

April eyed him with surprise. ''I thought you agreed to let me show you the real world we women live in?''

A wry smile quirked the corner of his lips. ''I did, I still do. I just figured you could point out my shortcomings on a river cruise as easily as anywhere else.''

''Now?''

''Why not?'' He gestured to the large window behind her desk. ''The sun is shining, the sky is blue and the air is clear. Enough to open a man's mind. That *is* what you had in mind when you offered to show me the real world, right?''

''Yes.'' April mentally calculated the odds of making Sullivan change his chauvinistic habits. ''That, and a few other things.''

Sullivan's eyebrows rose, and a calculating glint came into his eyes. Too late, April realized she'd echoed one of his earlier innuendos. Hers had been innocent. She wasn't so sure about his. What she was sure of was that after today she'd never be able to think of Sullivan as a stuffy academic again.

Lucas was intrigued by the way the fire lurking behind April's eyes grew brighter. The freckles that paraded across her nose had turned a dusty pink. He actually discovered that blushing freckles were a turn-on.

Did he really want to spend the next few hours with April debating the sociological aspects of the mating game? Or to debate his theory that the mating game was simply a question of mind over matter?

The professional side of him said yes. The male side of him that had discovered April's charms rebelled. Maybe it *was* time to smell the roses. Now that his academic research was behind him and the publication of his article guaranteed, there was no reason not to mix business with pleasure. "So, how about it?"

"If you think fresh air will help, sure," April said as she glanced at her shoes with her four-inch heels. "First, I have to go home and change into something more suitable for sightseeing. Where shall we meet?"

"Right here and right now," Lucas said. "How about I hitch a ride with you? It'll save both of us some time. I left my car at home for a tune-up and took the bus."

April considered the innocent look in his eyes. Who else but a college professor short on funds would choose a bus, instead of taking a taxi? Or had he intended to hitch a ride with her all along?

Yesterday, she'd thought him clueless about human behavior, but not now. Not after having seen him play last night, and not with the man he seemed to have become today.

Had Sullivan actually changed? Or was it her perception of him that had changed?

She reminded herself that she was Sullivan's editor, nothing else. That she was doing him a favor by offering to show him there was more to finding a genuine relationship, marital or otherwise, than by following a ridiculous set of rules.

She took a deep breath. "I'm ready. Are you?"

"Sure," he replied with a last look at her legs. "Since you know where you're going, you can drive. After you've changed into something more comfortable, I'll take things from there."

April's eyes narrowed as she led the way out of her office. *She* could drive? *He'd* take things from there? Which one of his rules called for her to let him take charge of the afternoon when the idea to open his mind to the real world had been her idea in the first place?

Boldly returning the covert glances of the women in the outer office, Lucas followed April to the elevator. What he'd done to turn her into an icicle just when they appeared to be getting along so well beat the heck out of him.

Hadn't he overlooked her candid remark about fighting the desire to laugh at what he'd written?

Hadn't he managed to keep his cool even after

April's suggestion he think about turning his work into a tongue-in-cheek offering to attract readers?

Of course, Eldridge's remark at lunch yesterday about anticipating a rise in circulation once Lucas's controversial article was published, instead of commenting on his professional approach, hadn't been easy to take, either.

If anyone should've been annoyed, it was Lucas himself.

One way or another, he thought as he followed April's swaying hips, cruising the Chicago River promised to turn into one hell of an afternoon.

THE STREETS IN THE Lincoln Park district of Chicago were lined with maple trees and apartment buildings. Antique streetlights, a sign of Chicago's past, stood at intervals, as did small, whimsical plaster statues of cows celebrating Chicago's famous fire.

April pulled to a stop in front of a three-story apartment house. She had already decided the safest course of action was to ask Lucas to wait for her in the car. Instead, before she could take her key out of the ignition, he was out of the car and holding the car door open for her.

Surprised, she hesitated before she started to swing her legs out of the car. To her dismay, she caught the heel of her left shoe on the car door frame and fell into his arms.

"I didn't mean to do that," she gasped when his arms tightened around her. "Sorry."

"I'm not," he replied with a smile. "It was my fault." Instead of letting April go, he steadied her in his arms. "Are you going to be okay?"

Ignoring an inner warning, April gave in to a desire she'd toyed with since she'd seen him at the Roxy—to be held in Sullivan's arms. She was right. His arms were sure and strong. The chest she'd last seen beneath an open black shirt was solid and warm. His velvet brown eyes shone with concern, and as his gaze locked on hers, with something else.

If it had been anyone other than this man holding her in his arms, she would have said her physical response to him was instinctive and natural. But this was Lucas Sullivan, the author of "Sullivan's Rules," aka "The Mating Game," chauvinist and egotist number one! Impossible!

"It depends on what you mean by okay." April pulled out of his embrace, tried standing and gasped at the pain that shot through her leg. "I think I've twisted my ankle."

"It's my fault. I should have been careful not to startle you when I opened the car door," he said, his arms carefully supporting her. "I've found that today's women generally prefer to do things for themselves."

April gazed up at him in disbelief, the throbbing in her ankle momentarily forgotten. "See? It's obvious you haven't lived in a world outside of academia if you can come up with such a ridiculous statement!"

"Come again?"

"In spite of what you think, women like to be cherished, like having men sometimes do things for them," she said. "Most of us respond to men who not only treat us as equals but are considerate, too."

"Ah! The independent woman versus the mating-game rules again?"

"You got it," she said, hopping on one foot. She was tempted to tell him that most women, independent or not, wanted someone to watch over her, emotionally. Still, having just declared her independence, it didn't seem like the right time to tell him so.

Lucas started to let April go when he noticed the fine line of pain on her forehead, the hint of moisture in her eyes. He glanced down to see her still standing on one foot.

"It looks as if you've really hurt yourself. Here," he said, "sit down for a minute while I check out the damage."

April winced and sank back down on the car seat. Lucas knelt, gingerly slid off her shoe and gently ran his fingers over her leg from her ankle to her knee.

"It's only my ankle that hurts," she said wryly when he started back down her leg. "The rest of me is just fine."

She could have sworn she'd heard him mutter, "I know." She gritted her teeth against the pain. "Finished?"

He cupped the heel of her foot in his hand and looked up at her. "I don't think you've broken anything,'' he said as he gently massaged her heel. ''Maybe a sprain... Here, try to move your ankle by yourself. Stop if it hurts too much.''

April took a deep breath and slowly slid her heel back and forth in Lucas's open hand. The friction of her nylons against his warm flesh sent a tingle up her leg. To her chagrin, the hormones she'd firmly set on the back burner months ago after being jilted at the altar began to stir.

Her gaze locked with Sullivan's, April realized it had been forever since she'd been touched so intimately. Even then, she couldn't remember responding to her erstwhile fiancé's touch the way she did to Sullivan's.

Jim's touch had been proprietary, his attitude toward starting a family, evasive. In retrospect, she realized Jim hadn't wanted children. All he'd wanted was a compliant trophy wife.

Sullivan's article might indicate he thought marriage was a bargain between two people and that sex wasn't of primary importance. He might even believe domestic and companionship qualities of a relationship were more important than good sex, but she wasn't sure he actually meant what he wrote. Not when he touched her like this.

She didn't know how Sullivan actually felt about marriage or children. From what he'd said, he'd been an only child. A child whose parents' sorry marital experience had turned him not only into a cynic but a poor potential marital partner.

Common sense told her to move on.

Her body didn't seem to be listening.

Rita had been so right. A mutual sexual attraction, even between two very different people like Sullivan and herself, was as normal as the sun rising in the morning and setting at night.

It was also out of the question.

Foot play was definitely out.

"I'm sure my ankle will be fine in a few minutes." She slid her foot out of Lucas's hand, gingerly tested standing and smothered a gasp of pain. "Thanks for your help. I'm sure I'll be okay in a few moments."

Lucas rose. "Better let me help you inside."

April reached into the car for her bag. Considering the way she was beginning to feel about this unexpected side of Sullivan, the last thing she needed was his arm around her. Or to know he was in the next room while she changed to something more appropriate for river cruising. "Are you sure you wouldn't rather wait for me here in the car? I won't take long."

He regarded her thoughtfully. "You look a little pale. I'd feel a lot better if I went with you upstairs. Besides," he said with smile that made her head swim, "you might change your mind about the river cruise once you're inside. You might want to stay in your apartment and talk there."

April wasn't sure if Sullivan was teasing her, but she couldn't quarrel with his reasoning that she needed help. Her ankle *was* still throbbing. "I won't change my mind. The cruise sounds inviting. The fresh air will do me good.''

Mentally crossing her fingers, she settled for leaning on his arm while she gingerly made her way to her apartment.

Once inside, April said, ''Make yourself comfortable. I won't be long.'' Then she disappeared behind a closed door.

By the time her panty hose were off, she heard the sound of the refrigerator opening, followed by the clinking of ice cubes.

She opened the bedroom door. ''What's going on?''

''I'm making you an ice pack,'' he called back. ''Why don't you get off your feet? I'll be with you in a minute.''

April sank down on the edge of her bed, the last place in the universe she should have been with Sullivan about to join her.

He appeared in the bedroom doorway, carrying a cold pack made from a kitchen towel wrapped around ice cubes. ''If you put your leg up on the bed,'' he said, ''I'll wrap this around your ankle. It'll make it feel better.''

''Thank you.'' April glanced around her. The bedroom door stood open, but Sullivan felt too close for comfort. ''I'll just rest here for a few minutes before I change, then. How about you wait in the living room outside?''

He hesitated at the foot of the bed. "Are you sure you can manage by yourself?"

She didn't like the speculative look in his eyes as he gazed at her. Or the way her body was answering him. "Yes, I'm sure. Please close the bedroom door behind you."

Lucas winked. "Holler if you change your mind."

He dodged the pillow she threw at him on his way out of the bedroom.

In the living room, Lucas noted with approval the laid-back decor with its feminine chintz and maple furnishings. He'd been right about April. There was more to her than her businesslike persona.

An upright piano beside a sunny window drew his attention. Just when he'd decided the reason for April's dim view of his research was that they had little in common, he discovered they both loved music! Although, he thought with a smile as he toyed with the keys and checked out the sheet music on the rack, their tastes were obviously very different.

Yet he certainly appreciated April's taste in music. Everyone was entitled to his or her own likes and dislikes. Everyone needed a way to unwind, free inner tensions. For him it was the electric guitar.

He picked up a recent copy of *Today's World,* idly leafed through the contents and frowned. Apparently his own article *was* different from the mix of articles in the issue. Where most of these articles seemed rather dull, his, at least in his opinion, was interesting.

Was dullness the problem Eldridge had with his magazine?

Tom might be using his article to bring the magazine to life, but he'd be damned if he was going to let anyone make him look like a fool.

He and April would have to have a serious talk about his article soon.

"Nice place you have here," he called after a while. It was the sort of warm home that a woman who followed the rules in his mating-game article might have created. So why did April pretend to be all business at the office when her nest said otherwise?

And what was taking her so long to change, anyway? "How you doing?" he called to the closed bedroom door. "Need any help?"

The door swung open. Dressed in a green-and-white bamboo-and-floral camp shirt and a matching short skirt, April stood on one foot leaning against the wooden doorframe. "I'm afraid my ankle still hurts."

Lucas dropped the magazine, strode across the room and bent down in front of her. "Here, rest your foot on my knee while I take another look."

April gingerly raised her foot and winced before she set it on his knee.

Lucas gently ran his hands over the injured ankle. "It *is* a little swollen. Got a tensor bandage?"

"I do, as a matter of fact. You'll find it in my

bathroom medicine cabinet.'' She laughed. ''Do I dare trust that you know what you're doing?''

''You forget that I'm a doctor,'' he said playfully. ''I learned how to treat twisted ankles in Sprain 101.''

She tried and failed to repress a grin. ''Don't you think we're a little too old to be playing doctor?''

''Not me. Where did you say the bandage was? Oh, yes, the medicine cabinet. Wait here. I'll be right back.''

Lucas made his way through the bedroom to the adjoining bathroom, noticing its faint lemony scent. A lacy cream-colored teddy—he believed that was what they were called—hung drying over the shower curtain rail. A reminder that his suspicions about the *real* April Morgan had been right. Under her smart professional persona, she wasn't the woman she pretended to be.

Any more than he was the man he appeared to be.

Looks could be deceiving, he thought after grabbing the bandage, then sliding back through her bedroom. One idle thought led to another. After he saw his work published, maybe he ought to take the time to smell the roses. With April? Highly unlikely, though when he thought of the lacy teddy, the notion held possibility.

But if he were to maintain a professional relationship with April, thinking sensual thoughts about her wasn't a good idea. Even though he was surrounded by temptation.

"Pardon me." Before April knew what Sullivan intended, he'd picked her up and carried her to the couch, where he set her down gently. "Here, give me your foot." He slowly wrapped the tensor bandage around her ankle and sat back. "There, that should help."

April wiggled her ankle. The tight bandage felt good, Sullivan's tender touch even better. "It does, thank you. Give me a minute to put on my sandals and we can leave."

"Are you sure you can walk on that ankle?"

"I'm sure," April said with a sigh as her stomach growled, "but I seem to have another problem."

"Bandage too tight? Here, let me look."

"No, I hate to admit it, but whenever there's a crisis, I get hungry." Her stomach growled in sympathy. "I sure could use a hamburger right now."

"Ah, comfort food," he said knowingly. "My first choice is usually a beer. Maybe we should stay here for a while to give your foot a rest and still satisfy ourselves. Now, what's in your refrigerator? If an omelet and a decent sandwich will substitute for a hamburger, I can do a hell of a job with both. How about it?"

April knew better than to test the growing attraction she felt for Sullivan by remaining in her apartment with him. She was about to turn down his suggestion when her stomach growled again.

"All right. You should be able to find what you need in the refrigerator. But we are not, repeat not, staying here for the rest of the afternoon. After we eat, we'll go."

"Okay," Lucas said with a shrug. Before she had a chance to protest, he picked her up again and carried her into the kitchen, where he sat her down in a chair. "There. Now sit there while I work some magic."

April frowned. She hadn't been carried around since she'd been a baby and she didn't appreciate it now. Not that she wasn't grateful for his attention—she was. She just wasn't too pleased with his take-charge attitude.

She watched as Sullivan surveyed the meager contents of the refrigerator. She usually saved grocery shopping for Saturday or Sunday afternoons, and today was Friday. Afraid to explain why she was almost out of food for fear he'd take charge of that, too, she silently waited for his reaction.

"Okay," he said, emerging from the refrigerator. "There's milk, four eggs, butter and some feta cheese and a green pepper." He studied the remains of a loaf of bread and shrugged. "The bread isn't fresh, but it'll do for toast. So unless you have any objections, there's a Sullivan special coming up."

"And after we have lunch?"

"No problem," he said as he took off his jacket and rolled up his sleeves, "there'll still be time to take a river cruise if you're up to it."

April watched as he pulled down a copper frying pan from the overhead rack and set it to warm before he added slices of green pepper. He found a mixing bowl in a cabinet and was actually humming by the time he cracked the eggs in the bowl, added milk and the cheese and briskly stirred the mixture together.

"Who would have thought you'd be so handy in a kitchen?" April said as she watched him go about the business of creating the omelet. "How good are you with cleaning up the mess you make?"

"No problem," he replied with a flourish of a wooden spatula. "I was largely raised by my strict father, remember, so without a woman around, I learned it was clean up after myself or I wouldn't get another meal."

April watched as he poured the egg-and-cheese mixture over the sautéed green pepper in the skillet. In the kitchen at least, he might be right about the importance of companionship. As for his experiences after his parents' divorce, no wonder his rules required for a woman to do the things for him he'd had to do for himself.

Thinking back to her own childhood, April remembered how her mother had waited on her sons hand and foot, while encouraging her daughter, April to do things for herself. The experience had turned April into an independent woman. Being jilted at the altar had finished the job.

She watched as Sullivan flipped the omelet in the pan with one hand while reaching to turn on the toaster with his other. The man might be misguided in his theories when it came to women, but it looked as if he had the right stuff when it came to cooking.

A man who was strong in a crisis and at home in a kitchen had to have desirable genes.

Chapter Five

Lunch over, the kitchen restored to its pristine condition, they prepared to leave for the marina.

''I'll drive,' Lucas said when she pulled her car keys out of her purse. ''Limping around your apartment on one foot is one thing, dealing with Chicago traffic with a sore ankle is another.''

April glared at him. The warm feelings she'd begun to have about him faded as the take-charge Sullivan reappeared. ''It's my left ankle that's injured. My car's automatic, so I don't need to use my left foot when I'm driving. What's the big deal?''

''Not that big, maybe. But why not take the opportunity to completely relax and let someone else do the work?'' He held out his hand for the car keys. ''C'mon. Hand 'em over.''

She tightened her hand on the key ring. No one was going to tell her what to do. ''Step aside, Sullivan. I don't intend to get into a debate with you over something as stupid as this.''

"Neither do I," he said quietly. "I'm doing this for your own good. Now, hand 'em over."

From the determined look in his eye, April recognized she was on the losing end of the argument. Logic was on his side, but she'd be darned if she'd give in without a tussle. He'd have to give a little, too.

"Only if you promise to stop trying to carry me everywhere we go," she said, scowling. "I might have had to lean on you on the way up here, but I can make it down on my own two feet."

He eyed her bandaged left ankle. "Even if it hurts?"

"Even if it hurts," she snapped, ignoring a sudden twitch of pain. "If I gave in to you now, I'd be no better than those women you describe in your article."

"Hardly," he said with a pointed look at the key ring in her hand. "You don't even come close."

"Just as long as you know it!" she answered. "For that matter, you're not the man I thought you might be under that academic exterior. After reading those ridiculous rules of yours, I'm not even sure you have any red blood in your veins." She peered at him. "Or are you just trying to annoy me?"

He threw up his hands in a gesture of defeat. "Not me! All I'm trying to do is to save you from yourself."

"When I need saving, I'll let you know," April muttered, placated for the moment, but not for long.

She was determined to bring Sullivan's thinking into the twenty-first century before he had a chance to turn her into a Sullivan woman. She planted her left foot on the kitchen floor and smothered a groan. "So what do you say? Do we forget the river cruise, or do we take advantage of a lovely afternoon?"

Lucas calculated the chances of persuading April to let him carry her to the car. Judging from the fierce look in her eyes, the answer was still no. Regrettable. He'd been looking forward to having her in his arms again.

She was womanly where a woman ought to be womanly, and her complex personality was one he looked forward to knowing better. Too bad she was so strong-minded; it made getting to know her difficult—too many walls to break through. Still, if he didn't give in to her now, the lessons might be over before they began. Although he probably should have been relieved, he couldn't stand the thought of not finding out what she was up to.

April Morgan might not be the ideal woman for a man's marital choice, he thought as he made up his mind to back off, but she had the makings of an interesting teacher.

"I ought to have my head examined," he finally muttered, "but, okay. Have it your way. Unless you ask for help, I promise to keep my hands off you. The keys, please."

"Only if you promise to try to keep an open mind for the rest of our time together."

"Deal," he answered, relieved he didn't have to wrestle her for the car keys. "I know the river cruise was my idea, but are there any other conditions attached to these lessons of yours?" Lucas asked. "Might as well get them all out on the table before we go any further."

"Not yet. Maybe later." She handed him the car keys and limped her way out of the apartment to the elevator.

Hoping she would give in and ask for help, Lucas took care to walk behind her, just in case. She was a handful, all right, he thought admiringly as he followed her swaying hips out of the elevator and to her car. As long as she wasn't trying to persuade him to make any changes to his article, there was no harm in spending some time in her company. All in the name of possibly learning something about life, of course.

April was listing to the right by the time they reached her car. He smothered a comment as he unlocked and opened the passenger door. "Okay if I help you in?"

She shot him a quelling look.

"No, I guess not." Lucas shrugged. "A promise is a promise. Go ahead, hop in."

Thankfully, the drive to the marina where the river cruise boats docked was short. April looked as if she was planning a mutiny while he was busy trying to figure out how to keep her too occupied to change her mind about those intriguing-sounding lessons of hers.

By the time the cruise boat was threading its way along the Chicago River, it was clear to Lucas that having April at his side, their thighs touching, was too distracting for him to learn *any*thing.

He'd been right about suggesting the cruise, though, he thought as he inhaled the clean afternoon air. At the moment, his article and its publication were the furthest thing from his mind.

The tour guide's informational spiel, including how Mrs. O'Leary's cow had inadvertently kicked over a milking pail and set the city of Chicago on fire in November 1871, wasn't helping him in his quest to know April better.

He finally gave up trying and sat back to idly survey his fellow passengers.

Across the aisle, a young woman was holding her hand up to the sun to admire her glistening diamond ring. The man beside her had his arm around her shoulders. A newly engaged couple?

Another young couple down from them were wrapped in each other's arms.

Lucas's gaze move on to a white-haired elderly couple sitting in the row in front of him. They were holding hands.

He was distracted in his survey by April's hair, auburn strands that kept blowing across his lips. Enchanted by their silken texture, he was almost reluctant to brush them away.

''Sorry about that,'' April said when she noticed. ''I should have brought something to tie back my hair.''

''I'm glad you didn't,'' he found himself saying. When she looked at him in surprise, he was lost in her eyes, sparkling pools of changing colors.

He'd thought April beautiful before, but she was breathtaking now.

Suddenly he remembered why they'd gone out today. ''I thought you were going to show me the real world,'' he said, shifting to put an inch or two of space between them for safety's sake.

''I already have. Look around you.'' April motioned to the assorted pairs of lovers. ''This is what I wanted to show you.''

Lucas dutifully checked out his fellow passengers one more time. ''Couples unable to keep their hands off each other?''

''That's called love, Sullivan!'' she retorted. She paused while a passing cruise boat blew its horn in a salute before she went on. ''They're all doing what comes naturally. And furthermore,'' she added, ''I doubt if they stopped to think why they were attracted to each other. Or that they stopped to consider a set of rules like yours before they decided they were.''

''Maybe not,'' Lucas agreed as the elderly man murmured to his wife and leaned over to gently kiss her forehead, ''but that doesn't mean they're all going to live happily ever after. Based on my research, that usually only happens in fiction. Somewhere along the line, rational people have to give rational thought to any relationship, especially marriage."

"Rational thought, my eye," April said as she remembered her earlier ill-fated attraction to Jim, definitely a misguided choice for a husband. "Take it from me, when it comes to the decision to get married, there's not much rational thinking involved."

Lucas waited until she wound down and, since she'd opened the door, finally asked the question he'd wanted to ask April all afternoon. "Haven't you ever wanted to get married, settle down and have children?"

For a moment, he thought she would tell him it was none of his business.

"Yes," April answered after a brief hesitation. "I did make it as far as the altar once."

No surprise there, Lucas thought. The surprise was why she hadn't gone through with the wedding if she'd gotten that far. "Want to talk about it? I'm told I'm a good listener."

If she hadn't sensed a genuine concern in his voice, April would have kept the story to herself. The man was a mind reader, a chameleon, changing personalities to suit the occasion, she thought as she considered him.

The last thing she wanted was to get personal with a man who didn't know beans about love. She'd be far better off to think of Sullivan as merely a name on the printed page, instead of a man she could talk to. And yet, he *was* easy to talk to. She gave in to the impulse to tell him about her ego-smashing rejection.

"My fiancé eloped with one of my bridesmaids moments before the wedding ceremony," she said, reliving the moment when her mother had handed her the brief note Jim had left behind him.

"Were you sorry?"

"No. Actually, I felt relieved. I'd already begun to feel something was wrong with our relationship, but I didn't have the sense to back out myself. You see, I'd wanted marriage, a husband and a father for my children, before my biological clock ran down." She shrugged, but a fine sheen of moisture appeared in her eyes before she turned away to gaze at the passing scenery. "I picked the wrong man. All Jim wanted was a playmate."

In spite of April's confession that she was glad her intended groom had deserted her, Lucas knew enough about relationships to realize that her experience must have been traumatic.

Still, after his own unhappy childhood, the idea of children had become a forbidden territory he didn't intend to visit. Clearly, April felt differently. "Are you still interested in having children?"

"The clock is still ticking," she said with a sigh. "But enough about me. How come you've never gotten married?"

Fair was fair. "I've already told you about my sorry family history. Dad's bitterness about marriage,

I guess, rubbed off on me. I decided a long time ago to concentrate on my studies and to leave marriage and procreation to someone else.''

''At least you have your music to remind you that you've got a human heart beating inside of you,'' she murmured.

''Yes, I suppose I do. In fact, I know I do.''

Lucas looked away. April had turned out to be the kind of woman he could share his most intimate thoughts with, and that came as a surprise.

''I suppose you could say we're two sides of the same coin,'' he said. ''One side avoiding matrimony and all that it entails and the other longing for marriage, a home and children.''

''I guess,'' April agreed as she reached behind her head and tried to tie her long hair in a knot. ''The truth is, that while I've always wanted to get married and have children, I'm still single.''

Lucas nodded. His question about what April was passionate about outside of her job had been answered. She might have an independent streak, but she was passionate about a home and a family. Husband included.

He'd suggested a river cruise to avoid having to talk about his study and the article Tom had commissioned. Now he was beginning to realize he'd missed something. He'd have to take another look at his original thesis and add a rule about children. Judging from the longing he glimpsed in April's eyes, it would have to be determined from a woman's point of view.

"Why spoil a beautiful day by dwelling on the past, Sullivan?" April said as the boat neared the marina. "Forget about yesterday. We came out here to educate you."

"Call me Lucas," he said with a rueful grin that almost knocked off April's socks. "This Sullivan is some other guy you're obviously not comfortable with, while I, Lucas would like to become friends. In fact," he continued before she could answer, "now that you've tried lesson number one on me, I'm not sure I'm comfortable with the guy myself."

Surprised, April's eyes widened. "Does that mean you've actually changed your mind about your article?"

"Nope," Lucas answered. "There's still the academic side of me to consider. To be honest, unless something happens to change my mind, I don't think I'm ready to change a thing. I just meant it might be easier for you to think of me as Lucas, the guy who plays the guitar."

April blinked. If she hadn't already discovered for herself there was more than one side to Sullivan, including an innate sensual side he didn't seem to be aware of, she would have been touched by his insight.

As for calling him Lucas, no way. In her present state of mind, she was sure she could manage his

Sullivan side—the methodical academic. It was the Lucas side of him she was in danger of falling for.

"So, you're actually suggesting we forget talking about the rules you describe in your article? I don't see how we can, not without discussing the meaning of love as opposed to the rational approach your rules imply."

Lucas looked into her eyes, the sort of eyes poets wrote about. Why spend the rest of the afternoon arguing about a subject neither of them were able to agree on when their time together was so limited? He thought again of more pleasurable ways they could use the time. "Maybe we should pass on both topics and talk about something else?" he suggested.

A child's voice sounded. "Daddy, Daddy! My balloon flew away!"

"I'll buy you another one, sweetheart," a laughing male voice answered. "Here, come and give Daddy a great big hug."

"Listen to that exchange, Sullivan," April commented, her thoughts turning to the touching picture of a man hugging a little girl as her father had held her. "There are all kinds of love, including the love of a parent for a child."

Lucas's eyes lit up. "Agreed."

"That's not the only issue here," April said, dismissing his smile. "I'm willing to concede there are many reasons behind the male-female attraction. But I haven't changed my mind—I don't believe in your rules for the mating game. I still believe that when we fall in love, we're subconsciously looking for a mate with strong genes to pass on to our children."

"That's only biology," he said, not for the first time. "If two people decide it's time to marry, there should be more than a physical attraction between them to make the marriage work. All you have to do is check out the latest divorce statistics."

"And there's your own sad experience, or rather, your father's, I suppose?"

"Yes, but that was a long time ago and doesn't matter anymore. I was speaking as a social scientist and in more general terms."

April realized that the more she learned about Sullivan, the easier it was to understand how he'd come up with his mind-boggling set of rules for the mating game.

"Okay, but when you do decide to marry," April continued, determined to prove her point, "I can't believe your wife will have to be the woman you describe in your study."

Lucas squirmed. She was getting closer to his way of thinking than she knew. "How I personally feel is irrelevant. Like I said, I'm not looking for a wife."

"Maybe," she suggested with an inviting smile, "after I show you the real world, you'll want to."

Lucas shrugged. He'd not only learned not to argue with April when her mind was made up, he had no intention of falling in love, marrying and having children, and risk having his heart broken like his father.

To further complicate matters, he couldn't tell April he was beginning to suspect that while he was sure his so called "rules" were empirically correct, perhaps the methods he'd used might have been faulty.

Uneasy at these unwelcome thoughts, he asked, "What comes next?"

"I'm not quite sure. I'll have to think about it," April replied as the cruise boat pulled into the marina. Before she could elaborate, a voice came over the loud speaker thanking the passengers for their patronage and inviting them to come back soon.

"I guess it's time to disembark." Holding on to the back of the seat in front of her, April tested her ankle and rose to her feet. "Thank you for an interesting afternoon."

Interesting? Lucas had the gut feeling that there were going to be far more interesting things to come. "Need some help back to the car?"

"No, thank you," April answered. "Actually, my ankle feels much better. Evidently, all I needed was to get off my feet for a little while. Hand over the keys. I'll drive this time."

A brown eyebrow rose. "With a bum left ankle?"

"Of course," April replied, her hand extended. "You'll see. I keep telling you, I can drive more easily than I can walk. Remember that tomorrow."

Lucas quietly handed over the keys. "What's going on tomorrow?"

"I'll pick you up in the morning at eight sharp.

Brace yourself, Sullivan. We start the rest of your lessons then. Trust me, you're going to enjoy every minute of the next few days."

"YOU'RE GOING TO DO WHAT?" Tom Eldridge stared at April as if she'd grown two heads.

"I said I'm going to take Sullivan to the company baseball game tomorrow," April repeated. "I don't want you to be surprised when we show up."

Tom's eyes narrowed and his complexion reddened. April half expected to see steam billow out of his ears. "With a view to what?"

"Getting Sullivan to take another look at his research and realize how faulty his conclusions are. Actually," April added earnestly, "I think he should go back to doing more research before you publish his article. As it reads right now, no woman in her right mind is going to buy the way he thinks women have to be in order to find a husband. Not without wanting to kick him in his shins."

"Hell no!" Eldridge surged to his feet, leaned over his desk and glared at her. "I forbid you to ask the man to consider changing his article, let alone one of his rules!"

Instinctively, April stepped back out of Tom's reach. "Come on, Tom. I thought you were serious when you said Sullivan and I ought to be able to work together. You must have realized how I felt about his thesis."

"Sure I did, but that's the point. It was a test,

April, merely a test,'' he sputtered. ''I wanted to see if your reaction would be the same as mine. Thank God, I was right,'' he said, looking pleased with himself. ''You were laughing while you read it! When I pretended to be impressed with Sullivan, I actually thought you were going to hand in your resignation.''

''You're right about that!'' she retorted. ''If I didn't have to pay the rent at the end of next week, I would have.''

''It might help you to know that I knew from the outset that Sullivan's work would get to you and all the magazine's female readers. That's the whole point. Take it from me, I didn't get this far in the magazine publishing world without trusting my gut.''

April was tempted to tell him he'd gone this far in the business because his father owned the magazine.

Sure, Tom was sharp, knowledgeable, hardworking and successful. Except that experience had taught her he was cut from the same chauvinistic cloth as most of the men she knew—Sullivans all.

''Are you telling me you're willing to risk the ridicule of the magazine-publishing world by publishing Sullivan's study the way he submitted it?''

''Hell yes!'' Eldridge rose and strode around his desk. ''Mark my words, April. Once the magazine hits the stands, it's going to cause a riot among our female readers while men will be laughing. Circulation figures are going to hit the roof! Before we're through tabulating circulation, our competition will turn green with envy!"

April stood her ground. "Sullivan may be misguided, but he's not stupid, Tom. After the way I've kept at him to consider making changes to the manuscript, if I back off now, he's bound to suspect something's fishy."

"That's precisely my point. You don't have to back off. All you have to do is to buy some time by insisting he take another look."

April's eyes narrowed. "While you go ahead and print it?"

"Sure. I've already told Sullivan I share his way of thinking. To tell you the truth, I actually do," Eldridge said with an embarrassed grin. "Maybe that's why I'm still single."

April frowned. "That doesn't sound ethical, Tom. Are you sure you want go ahead with this?"

"Like I said, the name of the publishing game is circulation numbers. I'm counting on you to keep Sullivan busy." He glanced at April's ankle. "What happened there?"

"I sprained it getting out of my car this morning."

"Here at work?" Eldridge asked, his smile gone. "Did you file a report of the accident?"

She might have known Eldridge was more interested in following government-mandated rules than worrying about her. When she got through with Sullivan, she vowed, she was going to work on him.

"No, at my apartment. I tripped when I was getting out of my car."

"Sorry to hear that." He eyed the bandaged ankle. "Bad enough to have to see a doctor, huh?"

"Not really," she said, without stopping to think. "Sullivan was there. It turns out he's a good man to have around in emergencies. He iced my ankle, then wrapped it for me."

Eldridge nodded his approval, but the look in his eyes was obviously on more than circulation figures. "Good, good. Sounds as if the two of you are getting along famously. So why are you back here talking to me, instead of sticking to him?"

April stood, ready to leave the office if Eldridge carried out the unspoken threat in his voice. "I intended to tell you about my plans to get him to change his mind. That is, before you told me yours."

"Plans?" Eldridge peered at her. "April Morgan, sometimes you scare me with your ideas. If your instincts about submissions weren't so good, I'd—" He broke off before he could complete his threat. "So, outside of the baseball game tomorrow, what other plans do you have in mind for Sullivan?"

April caught the calculating look in her boss's eyes. It made her uneasy, but considering the devious plans he seemed to have in mind for Sullivan, her own thoughts were better left unsaid for now.

"As I just told you, I want to try to show him the world we working women live in. Maybe even teach him a few mating-game rules of my own." April hesitated and worried her bottom lip. ''Now that you've told me what *your* plans are for him, it could be a waste of time. Are you sure I can't change your mind?''

''No, and not a word about this conversation to anyone, April!'' Eldridge warned. ''We both know Sullivan is a respected academic. We also know that the conclusions voiced in his manuscript are his, not ours. Bottom line, we're only publishing his article the way he wants us to and the way he submitted it to us. There's nothing wrong with that. If a few female readers out there happen to take offense, hell, it wouldn't be the first time and, hopefully, not the last. As far as I'm concerned there's nothing unethical in a healthy exchange of ideas.''

Torn, April had to agree. The integrity and reputation of his magazine were Tom's business. Sullivan's problem was his flawed article. Her problem appeared to be that somewhere along the line, Sullivan, biased or merely naive, actually believed in what he'd written and still needed her ''lessons.''

Even if its publication infuriated the magazine's readers and played right into Tom Eldridge's hands.

With Tom set on publishing ''Sullivan's Rules'' unchanged but for the title, it was obvious she couldn't save Sullivan from a riotous reader response even if she wanted to. He'd have to cope with the notoriety himself.

Lucas, Sullivan's alter ego, was another story. In the short period of less than two days, she'd discovered he had the potential to become a normal, well-rounded human being.

She wasn't sure what the future had in store for her, but she cared enough for the real Lucas to get him out of the line of fire before she moved on to her next project.

No matter what he said he believed in or what nonsense he submitted for publication, Sullivan was still a decent man who didn't deserve to be hurt.

Even if she thought of the man as a "Sullivan," read, chauvinist, or didn't think of him as marriage material for herself, she liked him enough to believe it was still her job to teach him a thing or two about women.

Chapter Six

With no response to the doorbell, April was poised to knock on the door of Sullivan's apartment when the door opened. A bleary-eyed Lucas Sullivan stood framed in the doorway. "April?"

Sullivan was definitely not a morning person.

Caught by surprise at his appearance, April blinked. He wore blue-and-white striped cotton pajama bottoms that hung low on the hips. His hair was tousled. The rest of him, including his feet, was bare.

It didn't take a big leap of April's imagination to realize that from his tapered waist to the tips of his toes Sullivan was all male. Gazing at his half-clothed figure made her body warm and her mind spin. Her reason for being here this morning was forgotten.

All she could think of was that Tom Eldridge could have had a deeper motive than circulation figures for suggesting she and Sullivan work together. Either that, or he and Sullivan had come up with the idea for reasons of their own.

One thing she was sure of was that Sullivan hadn't

had a clue his rules for the mating game were downright unrealistic where *he* was concerned. And that Rita's sexual-attraction theory had been right on.

This wasn't the first time she'd realized that there was more to Sullivan than met the eye. The first had been seeing him perform at the Roxy in his open black shirt and leather pants. Like now, she would never have believed the man capable of looking so sexy if she hadn't seen it with her own eyes.

Seeing his bare chest up close confirmed her first impression of him. He was one sexy male.

She tried an impersonal smile. "It's Saturday. Remember me?"

"Yeah, sure," he said, squinting in the early-morning sunshine.

First things first, April told herself. She wasn't about to test anyone's theory, especially Rita's. No matter how taken she might be with Sullivan's bare chest and toned muscles.

What she was here for was to help Sullivan test the accuracy of his conclusions by giving him a lesson in equality.

But at the rate her pulse was throbbing, she wasn't sure how far this attempt at enlightenment would go. Well, it was too late to worry about it. A baseball game waited.

She raised her eyes from the dark swirls of hair on his chest to meet his eyes. "Have you forgotten I promised to pick you up this morning?"

He covered a yawn with a hand and glanced at his

watch. "Sorry. I got in late last night." He grinned boyishly at her. "To tell you the truth, I'd hoped you'd forgotten your plans for me and that I could sleep in."

As if she could have forgotten a man like him! When the oceans dried up, but maybe not even then.

"No way," she said. "An agreement is an agreement."

He grimaced and rubbed sleep from his eyes. "What could you possibly have in mind at such an ungodly hour of the morning?"

"It's eight o'clock, Sullivan," she said, trying to be patient. "We don't want to be late. We're expected at a baseball game."

He groaned. "Who's crazy enough to want to play baseball this early in the morning on a Saturday? It's everyone's day off."

"Not ours. We're playing." She gestured to his bare chest and feet. "That is, we are as soon as you get dressed."

"*We* are?" Lucas's gaze lingered on April's lips before he moved on to a pristine white shirt tied in a knot at her trim waist. After a pause he moved on to an enticing expanse of velvet skin around her waist before he took in her misty-green pedal pushers. On her feet, she wore white sneakers. Her ankle, what he could see of it, was bare and slightly discolored from the sprain she'd gotten yesterday. The white baseball cap that held her hair away from her eyes signaled she meant business.

Although he wasn't prepared to say so yet, so did he. Only, the business he had in mind wasn't his article on the subject of marriage. Nor was it baseball.

He'd have to go along with April for now, but he guessed it didn't mean he couldn't have some fun along the way.

"I'd hoped you'd have something more interesting in mind than baseball for my enlightenment," he said, running his hand through his rumpled hair. "I'm no good at baseball or any competitive sports, for that matter. I've had my nose in books for years. The truth is, I haven't played since high school."

"No problem," April said as she shrugged off his excuses. "I'm sure you can pick the game up again. At any rate, the game isn't a competition between the sexes. We play for fun and exercise. You'll get into the spirit of things if you try. I'm going to umpire this morning and you can watch. What do you have to lose?"

"Ah," he said as her real reason for being here became clear, "lesson number two?"

Encouraged, April smiled brightly. "Now that lesson number one is behind us, you bet!"

Lucas took a long look at April before he gave in. Who would've guessed from seeing her in her office that she had such a carefree side? Not him. But baseball?

His profession was largely as a teacher, he reminded himself. Now that he had a chance to think about it, if someone was going to give someone else lessons, it was going to be him. He had a few lessons of his own he wouldn't mind teaching her....

And his lessons weren't about coed baseball.

To start with, he was tempted to pull her into his apartment and run his hands over the expanse of bare flesh around her waist. Then he wanted to kiss lips that were made to fit against his—not be wrapped around an umpire's whistle.

He was tempted to show her he was a red-blooded American male, and in spite of her sorry marital history, that she was all woman with needs of her own.

"So, how about it?" she said impatiently. "Are you coming with me or not? I don't want to miss the game."

"Yeah," he said reluctantly. "I have to shower and dress first." He rubbed the dark shadow on his chin. "A shave, too. A cup of hot, black coffee sure would help."

"If you have the makings, I can take care of that while you change," April said, happy again. "I usually pitch, but my ankle is a little sore this morning. And no," she said before he could suggest taking a look at it, "I don't need to be carried or have it wrapped again. It's just that it wouldn't be fair to the rest of the team if I tried to pitch. Like I said, I'm going to offer to be the umpire this morning. If you don't want to play, you can be my backup."

Visions of April with her tempting bare midriff running around bases swam before Lucas's eyes.

Thank goodness she was only going to umpire. Even so, he didn't know a man alive who could have kept his eyes and his mind on a baseball game when the umpire looked like her.

"Don't tell me you actually know enough about the game to umpire."

"Yes, of course. I played the game with my brothers for years at home. Why?"

Lucas's admiring gaze swept April. He couldn't tell her the truth without giving himself away. "You don't look the type. Besides, men are usually umpires."

"That's part of your problem, Sullivan," she retorted. "Women come in all shapes and sizes. We have the same dreams and ambitions as men do, including officiating at ball games. Except for possibly the women you describe in your study, there's no such thing as the stereotype you describe in your article. Given a woman's natural inclinations, and I should know in spite of what you think of me," she said, fixing him with a stern look, "I sincerely doubt the woman you're looking for actually exists."

"Interesting theory," Lucas muttered, grateful she had no way of knowing what he was thinking. He glanced over her shoulder. His next-door neighbor, Joe Rudin, was making a show of putting a leash on his bulldog and looked about to fall on his rear.

Lucas knew better. Rudin was busy eyeing April. An unexpected twinge of possessiveness hit him square in his gut. His eyes narrowed. For better or worse, April, at least for the duration of their business association, belonged to him.

"Why don't we take this argument inside?" He held open the door. "Come on in and make yourself comfortable while I shower and change."

He gave an inward sigh of exasperation when he saw Rudin's eyes light up.

Before he could stare Rudin into purgatory, April stepped by him and into his apartment. "Point me in the right direction and I'll make the coffee while you get ready. Hurry. The other ball players will be waiting for us."

"They'll have to keep on waiting," Lucas said, closing the door behind her. "I'd like to remind you one more time that I know squat about playing baseball. Besides," he added as he hitched up his pajama bottoms and led the way to what the landlord laughingly called a kitchen, "what is there about a baseball game that could possibly 'enlighten' me?" To his chagrin, the pajama bottoms slid back down his hips. He colored.

April turned her gaze away. "Lesson number two is going to be a lesson in equality. In baseball, at least in the kind we play, every player is equal but different. Women players don't have to impress the men, and vice versa. Believe it or not, it *is* possible to play for fun."

As she spoke, Lucas thought back to high school when he'd been young and stupid enough to try to impress a girl he'd admired. He'd stepped cockily up to the plate and hollered at the pitcher, ''Okay, pal, this one's going all the way to the moon,'' and then had struck out. He struck out again, when he was next at the plate, and the coach had pulled him from the game. The embarrassment he'd felt then wasn't worth remembering.

Now he was expected to play baseball with women so he could fall on his rear in front of April? He never should have agreed to her lesson plan without knowing up front just what she had in mind.

''Go ahead,'' he said, resigned to the inevitable. He pointed to a coffeemaker, already plugged in and timed to turn on at 10:00 a.m. Hell, it was barely eight. If he had the sense he was born with, he'd thank April for her good intentions, send her away and go back to sleep. Playing guitar in his rock band last night had taken a lot out of him, but judging from the way his body was responding to April, obviously not enough.

''Just turn on the coffeemaker,'' he repeated. ''It's ready to go. I'll be with you in a few minutes.''

Judging from his article, April might not think he knew much about women, he thought as he headed for the safety of a cold shower, but she had a lot to learn about testosterone. Trying to impress the opposite sex maybe came with the territory. But he'd be damned if he'd make a fool out of himself in front of her.

''So it's back to disproving my original study, is it?'' he called over his shoulder.

"You got it," April said as she turned on the coffee and surveyed the tiny kitchen. Outside of a few boxes of cereal, a few cans of soup and beans, the cupboards were bare. The refrigerator, as she checked for milk for her coffee, held several cartons of Chinese takeout.

In the living room, shelves of CDs and sound equipment covered one wall. The electric guitar Sullivan had played rested on a stand, another lay on the floor. Shelves filled with books lined another wall. More books overflowed on to the couch and coffee table. A desk by a window held a computer, a monitor, a printer and stacks of paper. Not a flat surface in sight to eat on even if he wanted to.

"What and where do you eat, for heaven's sake?" April called.

Lucas reappeared in the doorway with a bath towel around his waist. "If you're really interested, it's usually a sandwich or some kind of takeout. As to where, anywhere there's room."

"But I know you can cook. So why don't you cook for yourself?"

"I don't want to take the time. Too much else to do."

April was too busy staring at Lucas to really care where or what he ate. Not when he was draped in a towel that started low on his hips and ended at his bare mid thigh.

She averted her eyes. "That sounds like a man who thrives on research," she muttered as she surveyed the cluttered room. "On the other hand, maybe that's why you've managed to come up with those ridiculous rules of yours."

He paused in the doorway. "Because I don't have a kitchen table to eat on?"

"No. It's more than that." She laughed, tickled by the mock surprise on his face. She gestured to what appeared to her to be a stack of well-thumbed questionnaires. "You're not eating properly. Since you aren't looking for a wife, Sullivan, my advice to you is do yourself a favor and hire a maid."

Lucas was about to tell her hiring someone to cook for him wouldn't be half as satisfying or as interesting as a wife—when he noticed the glint in her eye. She was putting him on, and like a jerk, he'd risen to the bait. "As I said before, Ms. Morgan, I'm not looking for a wife any more than you're looking for a husband."

Hell, Lucas thought as he watched April turn back to the coffeemaker. The academic side of him might have taken umbrage at her blunt observations, but the more human side of him had to admire her honesty.

His first impression of April Morgan had turned out to be right on, after all, he mused wryly as he turned to go back and shower. As a challenge and a worthy opponent, there wouldn't be any dull moments. As for a playmate… "Go ahead, amuse yourself. I'll be back for coffee in five minutes."

Hiding a grin, he headed for the bathroom,

dropped the towel and turned on the water. April Morgan was beautiful, feisty, quick on the uptake and clever enough to keep him on his toes. Or, to use the language of his students and fellow band members, cool. He found himself humming as he stepped under the shower.

April frowned when Lucas disappeared. Amuse herself? That sounded too patronizing and chauvinistic for her to ignore. If there really *was* another side of the man, an educatable side, which she was beginning to doubt, it looked as if she had her work cut out for her.

"ABOUT TIME YOU SHOWED UP, April." Lyle Kirby, the chief organizer of the magazine's baseball games, grumbled forty-five minutes later. Until he noticed Lucas and then his eyes lit up. "New hire?"

"No, a visitor. Lucas, I'd like you to meet Lyle Kirby. Lyle is the sports editor of our magazine and doubles as our coach. Lyle, this is Lucas Sullivan. Sullivan is a new contributor to the magazine."

"Too bad," Kirby said as he shook Lucas's outstretched hand. "Anyone ever tell you you've got the grip of a born pitcher?"

Lucas smiled modestly. "Thanks, but I'm happy to leave the pitching honors to April. I'm just here this morning as an observer."

"That reminds me, Lyle," April broke in. "I sprained my ankle yesterday. I won't be able to do justice to the pitcher's job today. How about I take over as umpire?''

''Hi, April, Sullivan.'' Rita Rosales, the no-holds-barred woman Lucas had met in April's office, trotted up to join them before Lyle could reply. She glanced at Lucas's beige Dockers and crisp tan shirt with frank admiration. ''Lookin' good! Are you sure you want to play ball in that gorgeous outfit?''

Lucas found himself smiling at Rita. If April hadn't already filled him in about her, he would have believed all of April's friends were in on the crusade to humanize him. ''No. I'm just here as an observer. I'm not very good at the game.''

Rita's admiring gaze continued to roam over him. ''No problem. I'm willing to teach you,'' she said archly. ''All you have to do is ask.''

Lucas chuckled. ''I'm actually doing you all a favor by saying no.''

''If you change your mind—'' Rita rolled her eyes and gave an exaggerated sigh ''—just holler. I won't be far away.''

Bringing Sullivan to the baseball game was like offering honey to bees, April thought darkly as she spotted a determined Tiffany heading in their direction. Thank goodness Lili had taken the twins to the dentist, or even she, the shy one of the three of them, would have been eyeing Lucas. Not that she would have blamed her. She could hardly keep her own eyes off him.

''Lay off with the jokes, Rita. Sullivan is liable to

get the wrong idea about you. Rita usually displays more restraint,'' she told Lucas with a sidelong frown at her unrepentant friend. ''Although to listen to Rita carry on, you wouldn't know it.''

''Lyle,'' April said as she ignored Rita's grin, ''how about having Rita pitch in my place this morning?''

Kirby shrugged. ''Sure, since she's the only other decent pitcher on the staff. How about it, Rita?'' At her nod, he handed her the pitcher's mitt.

April wasn't through trying to keep Lucas from winding up knee-deep in admirers. ''How about using Tiffany for outfield? She's not bad at catching fly balls.''

Kirby shrugged again. ''That's as good a place to keep her out of trouble as any. I'll be the catcher. Let's get started before it gets too hot to play.''

April held out her hand for the umpire's whistle.

Lucas, standing well out of the line of fire, smothered a grin. He watched with interest while the magazine's staff, obviously following their weekly custom, chose sides and split into two teams of nine each.

To his amusement, it appeared from what April had explained on the way to the baseball diamond, each player chose a new position each game they played. It was a way to avoid undue rivalry or hurt feelings, according to April. Every player, man or woman, had equal value, she'd told him pointedly. As far as he could tell by the time she was through explaining strategy, the game was intended as a lesson in democracy—untalented female players got as much of an opportunity to play as talented male players.

Lucas didn't know if April had been the one who had come up with such a cockamamie set of rules. As far as he was concerned, a baseball game was by its very nature competitive. Without competition, the game couldn't be much fun, and certainly wasn't like any baseball game he'd ever seen. Unless April had set it up this way for his benefit, it was just another name for communal exercise.

This was supposed to be lesson number two?

April blew her whistle. "Play ball!"

The players scattered around the diamond. On the pitcher's mound, Rita cast a wary eye at the batter, Jenny from Sales, wound up and let loose a slow underhand lob.

"Strike one!"

Rita wet her lips, wiped her hands on her pink shorts, wound up and pitched another lob.

"Strike two!"

Rita grinned and pitched again.

"Ball one!"

"Come on, April," Rita protested, her smile replaced with a frown as she strode to home plate. "That was right over the plate. It should have been strike three! Jenny's out!"

"Nope. I'm the umpire here. It was ball one," April insisted.

"Lucas!" Rita called. "You've been watching. That was a strike, wasn't it?"

Lucas managed to look noncommittal. It was April's call, her close friendship with Rita forgotten in the heat of the game. Since it was going to be the only game he planned to attend, he didn't want to get caught up in any arguments. The umpire, and rightly so, he believed, was boss.

This was supposed to be a lesson in democracy?

For his money, what the game did demonstrate was that in the game of life everyone was accountable to someone.

Rita threw up her hands and stalked back to the pitcher's mound.

April blew her whistle again and the game continued.

In spite of April's efforts to be fair, it wasn't long before Lucas saw her heading to the pitcher's mound to confront Rita. Curious to see April's theory in action, Lucas followed at her heels.

To Lucas's surprise, Tom Eldridge, who had been making himself scarce in the audience until now, tramped on to the baseball field. "Come on, April. Give it a rest. With you out of the game, Rita is the only woman on our side willing and able to pitch. If you two keep arguing, one of you has to go. Since you're the one with a sore ankle," he said as he eyed her bare leg, "you know which one that is."

"Come on, Tom," April protested. "I call each pitch the way I see it."

"That's the problem," Tom growled. He took April's whistle out of her hand and pointed to the stands. "You're out as umpire, April. You want to watch, okay, but you're not going to call the shots." He motioned to Lucas. "You're in!"

"Thanks, but no thanks." Lucas backed away. "For one thing, I don't know anything about baseball."

"Then what the hell are you doing on the field besides getting in the way?"

Lucas wasn't about to tell Tom the game was supposed to be lesson two. Or that he intended to stay on April's good side for the duration of his enlightenment—for reasons of his own. He'd seen more than one baseball game on television where the umpire wound up being the target of rotten eggs, tomatoes or worse.

Especially now that Tom's authoritative action blew April's theory about everyone being equal on the playing field to hell.

Lucas took another cautious step backward. He was man enough not to want to confess he was here only because of April's challenge. And man enough to want to protect her from Tom's wrath. For a moment, he couldn't think of an answer that wouldn't sound ridiculous. "I'm testing a theory?" he said tentatively.

"Whose theory?" Tom scowled. "Yours?"

Lucas couldn't tell Tom they were testing April's theory about equality. She was in deep enough trouble with her boss already. He also didn't like the way the angry look in Tom's eyes turned calculating. He knew from their college days that some devious plan was going through the man's mind. A plan Lucas wasn't so sure he wanted to hear even if Tom had been willing to share.

"You're not being fair, Tom," April broke in.

"I'm not?" Tom glowered. "In case you've forgotten, I'm the boss around here."

"Back at the office, maybe, but not here," April declared before Lucas grabbed her arm and pulled her away.

"Enjoy the game, people," Lucas said. "April, I don't know about you, but I'm outta here."

"Take her with you and get her outta my hair." Tom beckoned to April with a grin. "She's all yours."

Lucas liked the sound of that, but he wasn't sure how an independent woman like her would feel about being passed on to his care as if she were a possession. Certainly not after the way she'd taken offense at his article.

"Looks as if your lesson backfired," he told her as he led her off the field. He was afraid that if he let go, she'd charge back to confront Tom again.

"Maybe," April muttered with a backward glance at the baseball diamond. "But don't get the wrong idea. Baseball may be out, but I'm not through with you yet."

As far as he was concerned, the argument at the

baseball field was a bit suspect, Lucas thought as he led a fuming April to her car. Tom had looked too pleased when he'd ordered April off the field. He should have been fuming.

Lucas wondered if he should warn her about Tom's little plots and schemes. He'd seen plenty of them back in their university days, and most of them backfired.

If only he could believe that April's behavior and Tom's earlier offer to have them work together weren't just part of a setup to use his mating-game article in ways he hadn't intended.

He carefully opened the car door for April. ''Better watch your ankle.''

She winced and slid into the driver's seat.

''Now might be a good time to hear lesson number three,'' Lucas said, more to divert her attention from the ball game than to expose himself to future lessons. ''Incidentally,'' he added, ''I hope it's not going to be something physical. I'm still beat from last night.''

Mentally visualizing him dancing across the stage, April could believe it.

April's cell phone rang before she had a chance to drive out of the parking lot. Frowning, she pulled the phone out of her bag. ''April here.''

Her eyes grew wider as she listened. ''No way! I don't care what... No! I can't. This isn't the time to talk. Can't this wait until Monday?''

Muttering to herself, she listened for another few

seconds, then folded the small phone and put it back into her purse.

"Disturbing news?"

"Nothing I can't handle." With a backward scowl over her shoulder, April stepped on the gas and shot out of the parking lot.

Lucas grabbed the door handle and hung on for dear life. "Where to next?"

"I'm going to find a hamburger, the biggest, juiciest hamburger I can find," she said grimly. "It's the only thing I can think of that helps calm me down when I get this upset."

She couldn't tell Lucas that being ejected from the ball game without just cause wasn't the only thing that had upset her. It was Tom's cell-phone call reminding her he expected her to make sure Sullivan's article resulted in a high-stakes, cutting-edge debate between Sullivan and her—and most of the female readers—about how to play, and win, the mating game.

Chapter Seven

''April,'' Lucas gasped as she burned rubber going around a corner. ''Whatever you have in mind isn't going to work. I have a better idea than a hamburger to make you feel better.''

''Take it from someone who's been there, done that, that there's *nothing* like a trip to the golden arches to cure what ails me,'' she said grimly. ''Especially if it comes with a side of fries.''

''Bet you a nickel!''

The size of the bet was so comical, April broke into laughter. ''A whole nickel?'' When he nodded, she pumped the brake to slow the car. ''You got it! But this had better be good, or I'm never going to let you forget it.''

The car finally slowed to the legal speed limit. ''So, what's better than a Big Mac?''

''It's a surprise,'' he answered. Color came back into his lips and he relaxed his grip on the door handle. ''Just drive to your office and I'll take it from there.''

A surprise to make her feel better? At her office? Clearly it was the softer, more enlightened side of Sullivan talking. Maybe he'd finally gotten her message that men and women were equal, only different.

"I want to apologize for the morning ending this way, Sullivan," she said as she maneuvered through uptown Chicago's traffic. "Everything was going along just great until Tom got into the act."

"If you intended the game to be another lesson in the possibility of male-female equality, it didn't quite come off," Sullivan said, admiring the confidence and self-possession with which April appeared to handle everything. Except for the baseball game.

She frowned. "We were doing great until Tom got into the act."

Lucas knew better than to disagree with her. From what he'd seen, the game had been a lesson in futility. "Maybe you should have used another example," he said as a peace offering. "Frankly, in this real world of yours you keep talking about, there's not much coed sports competition."

April frowned as a passing motorist sounded his horn. Instead of speeding up, she held her hand out the window and motioned for him to pass. "Keep the word *possible* in mind, Sullivan. This morning was only lesson number two. Like I said, I'm not through with you yet."

Sullivan blinked at the reminder. He was beginning to feel uneasy at the way April continued to call him Sullivan, a subtle reminder of how strongly she felt about him and his mating-game study, let alone his current article. ''You mean there's a lesson number three?''

''Yes, and maybe four and five.''

Sullivan swallowed a groan. The prospect of further lessons wasn't what was really bothering him—he'd gotten through the first two lessons and he would get through the rest. What *was* bothering him was the call April had taken on her cell phone, her distress as she'd listened and the mad dash for comfort food afterward. There had been more to the call than she was willing to share.

''I get the feeling that Tom's ejecting you from the game isn't the only reason you're upset, April. If we're gong to work together, how about leveling with me? What's going on here, anyway?''

April turned into the Riverview's underground parking and into her reserved parking space. ''Like I said before, it's not important!''

Lucas knew better. Whatever April had heard over the phone had shaken her. From the way she'd kept glancing at him out of the corner of her eye while taking the call, he was damn sure the conversation concerned him.

''Come on now,'' he said when the silence between them grew too deafening to ignore. ''It looks to me as if you could use a cool and objective person to talk to.''

''Meaning you?''

''Yeah, meaning me.''

Seeing the calculating look on April's face, he thought she was going to take him up on his offer. Instead, she shrugged and slid out of the car. "It'll keep. Right now, you owe me a surprise, Sullivan. I'm ready to collect—unless you've changed your mind?"

Lucas knew enough to put his offer—to listen to her bare her heart—aside for a more favorable time. What he had in mind now was bound to help.

"Lead the way," April muttered.

Inside the elevator, April held her hand over the control panel and looked at Sullivan. He was standing so close to her she felt caught up in the sheer animal magnetism of his body. So much for his rules.

"Where to?"

"The executive dining room, please."

"The *executive dining room?*" April's hand remained poised over the twentieth-floor button. "*That's* your surprise? What made you think it's better there than at McDonald's?"

"Wait and see." He reached over her shoulder and punched the button.

Leon, the longtime maître d', greeted April with a warm smile and an inquiring glance at Lucas. "Ah, Ms. Morgan. Are you and your guest joining us for an early lunch today?"

April smiled at the man who knew about her weakness for chocolate soufflé and periodically sent one down to her office. "Mr. Sullivan is a recent contributor to our magazine."

"Of course. This way, please." Leon led the way to a table for two by a sunny window overlooking the river, handed them leather bound menus and signaled for a waiter.

The waiter, Rick, smiled his welcome as he placed frosted glasses filled with water and lemon quarters on the table. "Are you ready to order or shall I come back later?"

April handed back the menu. "I already know, thanks. I'll have a Cobb salad, without the bacon bits. Easy on the dressing, please."

"And for dessert? The usual?"

April smiled ruefully. "Not today, thanks. I'm watching my weight."

Lucas peered over his menu. He liked the way April's lips curved when she smiled, the glint of pearly teeth, the hint of dimples playing hide-and-seek in her cheeks. As for having to watch her weight, no way, he thought. "Is that really all you're going to eat?"

"Yes. Why?"

"I thought you were dying for a hamburger?"

"Not here, Sullivan," she said with a glance at Rick. "Maybe later."

The waiter glanced inquiringly at Lucas. "And you, sir?"

"I'll have a Reuben sandwich, light on the sauerkraut. Coffee, black, please."

"Dessert?"

Lucas made a show of studying the menu before

he handed it to the waiter. ''A chocolate soufflé, with two spoons, please.''

Rick grinned. ''Got it!'' He picked up the menus and disappeared into the kitchen.

April smiled her pleasure. ''You've turned out to be quite a surprise, Sullivan. You remembered that the chocolate soufflé served here is my favorite dessert. I'm impressed.''

If the Sullivan side of him hadn't been warning him he was about to slide into dangerous territory, he would have told April there wasn't anything about her he was likely to forget. Not her enchanting hazel eyes, not her tumble of auburn hair glinting in the sunlight coming through the window behind her, not her predilection for hamburgers as comfort food. And certainly not her gorgeous smile.

What was becoming too clear was that his attraction to April was starting to get in the way of rational thinking. Not about his article, heaven forbid, but the apparent truth that April wasn't the woman he'd described in it.

The academic side of him cautioned him to remember her disagreement not only with his research methods, but with its conclusions.

All things considered, April Morgan should be the last woman he was interested in. but it was too late. He was already in danger of falling head over heels in lust with her. Considering their intellectual differences, it was a bad omen.

''No big deal,'' he answered casually. ''I just happened to remember you mentioned your favorite dessert when we first met. Since you didn't want one of your own, I figured sharing mine wouldn't hurt.''

''I wanted one,'' she said with that gorgeous smile. It had a way of breaking down his resolve to treat her to lunch and then be on his way. ''I've learned from sad experience that indulging in any kind of chocolate only adds to the waistline. A salad seemed a wiser choice.''

Sullivan eyed April appreciatively. Although her blouse now hung loosely around her waist, he had no trouble recalling the firm tanned skin of her midriff and her lush curves. She would have looked like a young girl masquerading as a grown woman if those curves hadn't given her away.

April was aware of Sullivan's admiration, and it made heat curl in her belly. She found herself thinking about the way he'd looked this morning with only a towel at his waist, the way he'd looked at the Roxy, where his performance had been physical in more ways than one. His movements on the stage while he played guitar and sang had sent her hormones into a frenzy.

Not that she could remember just what he'd been singing about at the time. What she *did* recall very clearly was the way he'd turned his back on the audience and gyrated his hips in the best rock-and-roll tradition.

Telling herself she was crazy for even thinking about Sullivan as a sensual man, April turned to her salad, which Rick had just placed before her. The mouthwatering scent of the fried onions in Sullivan's juicy Reuben sandwich wafting across the table made her salad taste like straw. When he reached for the ketchup, she sighed softly.

Sullivan must have heard her, because he silently put a small mound of fries on a small bread plate and slid it toward her. The bottle of ketchup followed.

April smiled her thanks. "I'm afraid you know all my weaknesses now."

"A hamburger, fries and a chocolate soufflé? Hardly worth mentioning," he replied, clearly amused. "Are you sure that's the whole list?"

"All I'm willing to confess to." She grinned and eyed his plate. "Oh, wait a minute! There *is* one more. Are you planning on eating that piece of watermelon?"

Lucas forked over the melon. "Someday when we get to know each other better, maybe I'll tell you about my own weaknesses."

Her grin broadened. "I wouldn't have thought a disciplined academic like you would have any weaknesses."

"That's only the academic side of me," he agreed cheerfully. "The other side...well, that's another matter."

April munched happily as she recalled his other weaknesses. "Time will tell, won't it?" She eyed his plate. "Aren't you going to eat the rest of your fries?"

Lucas pushed his plate to within her reach. "Be my guest. Just remember to leave room for dessert."

The soufflé, still warm in its small pot and dusted with powdered sugar, arrived. Lucas handed April a spoon, waited until she dug in, then joined her.

To his secret satisfaction, sharing the rich dessert turned into a game of dueling spoons. It didn't take him long to begin to envision the spoons as two bodies making love against pristine bedsheets.

He dropped his spoon and reached for his glass of ice water, hoping a swallow would cool him off. Maybe it was time to question April about the cellphone call.

"So," he began as Rick refilled his coffee cup, "do you feel better now? Ready to talk?"

April licked a small dab of chocolate off her spoon. "Mmm."

"I take it that's a yes?"

"I'm getting there, Sullivan," she said after another nibble at the soufflé. "So, what do you want to talk about?"

He took a deep swallow of coffee to take his mind off making love to April and using chocolate in ways that made his nether regions come to attention. "I'd like to know about that telephone call you took. And, more to the point," he added, "just what's going on between you and Tom that's disturbing you so?"

"Tom?" April eyed the empty little pot, sighed

The Harlequin Reader Service® — Here's how it works:

Accepting your 2 free books and mystery gift places you under no obligation to buy anything. You may keep the books and gift and return the shipping statement marked "cancel." If you do not cancel, about a month later we'll send you 4 additional books and bill you just $3.99 each in the U.S., or $4.74 each in Canada, plus 25¢ shipping & handling per book and applicable taxes if any.* That's the complete price and — compared to cover prices of $4.75 each in the U.S. and $5.75 each in Canada — it's quite a bargain! You may cancel at any time, but if you choose to continue, every month we'll send you 4 more books, which you may either purchase at the discount price or return to us and cancel your subscription.

*Terms and prices subject to change without notice. Sales tax applicable in N.Y. Canadian residents will be charged applicable provincial taxes and GST. Credit or debit balances in a customer's account(s) may be offset by any other outstanding balance owed by or to the customer.

If offer card is missing write to: Harlequin Reader Service, 3010 Walden Ave., P.O. Box 1867, Buffalo NY 14240-1867

BUSINESS REPLY MAIL

FIRST-CLASS MAIL PERMIT NO. 717-003 BUFFALO, NY

POSTAGE WILL BE PAID BY ADDRESSEE

HARLEQUIN READER SERVICE
3010 WALDEN AVE
PO BOX 1867
BUFFALO NY 14240-9952

yes! I have scratched off the silver card. Please send me my *2 FREE BOOKS* and *FREE mystery GIFT*. I understand that I am under no obligation to purchase any books as explained on the back of this card.

354 HDL DZ5Y   154 HDL DZ6F

FIRST NAME   LAST NAME

ADDRESS

APT.#   CITY

STATE/PROV.   ZIP/POSTAL CODE

(H-AR-06/04)

Twenty-one gets you **2 FREE BOOKS** and a **FREE MYSTERY GIFT!**

Twenty gets you **2 FREE BOOKS!**

Nineteen gets you **1 FREE BOOK!**

TRY AGAIN!

Offer limited to one per household and not valid to current Harlequin American Romance® subscribers. All orders subject to approval.

▼ DETACH AND MAIL CARD TODAY! ▼

and set down her spoon. ''You really mean you want to know what's going on between you and me, don't you?''

''Caught!'' he said ruefully. He'd already learned April was as sharp as she was attractive, but he hadn't realized he was so transparent. ''I should have known you'd be able to read my mind. Since I have a feeling the cell-phone call from Tom concerned me, the answer is yes.''

Around them, people began filtering into the dining room. After a quick glance at the newcomers, April nodded. ''In a nutshell, Tom wants us to engage in a ''cutting-edge'' debate after the publication of your article. He said he wants to see fireworks. He wants to cash in on the controversy he sees coming over your article.''

Lucas stirred. Fireworks? Heck, they had fireworks between them now, didn't they, if of a different kind? ''Are you sure that's what Tom meant?'' he asked cautiously

''Yep.''

Lucas's opinion of his old friend went down a notch. He'd been pleased at having been asked to write the article, but he never would have believed Tom would turn its publication into some sort of publicity stunt. ''Well, do *you* have a problem with that?''

''Well, I'm not delighted about the idea,'' she confessed. ''Tom wants us to debate our differing viewpoints on male-female relationships in a series of articles in the issues following the one your article appears in.''

Lucas remembered Tom's glee at what he'd called a probable negative female reaction to his article. ''I take it he intends my article to be unedited, left just as I wrote it.''

''Yes. He believes that as the author you have every right to expect to have it published without changes. No wonder he admires you,'' she added with a scowl. ''He's just as bad as the rest of you male chauvinists. If you don't mind my saying so, anyone who believes that drivel is another 'Sullivan.'''

The academic side of Lucas wasn't too happy at being called a male chauvinist. Or that he'd apparently lent his name to men who shared his point of view.

''I'm afraid the idea of debates is going to be a problem,'' he said after a few moments' thought.

April felt hopeful. If he wasn't interested in defending his article, she wouldn't have to worry about having to disparage it. ''You mean you're not interested?''

''No, that's not the problem. I could possibly be persuaded to debate my conclusions with you. The real problem,'' he said, ''is that you haven't had a chance to really understand my viewpoint and we haven't gotten to know each other well enough to enter into a meaningful exchange of ideas.''

''Well, then, maybe after a few more lessons, we

will be able to debate each other,'' April said with a wry smile. ''Are you game?''

Lucas stepped up to the challenge. Any way to get to know April better was okay with him. ''I am if you are.''

''Then we have no problem,'' she said, wiping her lips. ''After all, we're only talking about a debate on two different theories regarding the 'right' mate—the instinctive search for strong genes versus rational thinking. Although,'' she added with a wicked smile, there's also Rita's theory that sexual attraction is the way to go. I suppose we should consider *all* the theories.''

Lucas tried not to betray his personal interest in Rita's theory when it came to April. Rita might be right on when it came to dating, but to consider sexual attraction as the main basis for marriage? Hardly. Not when he'd learned from his parents' marital disaster that sexual attraction didn't last long enough to raise their son.

Which brought him back to the validity of his research of the mating game. If and when it came time to acquire a wife, at least he had his rules to fall back on.

''Are you suggesting we include your friend Rita in our debates?''

April laughed. ''Hardly. Like I said before, I'm sure it's all talk.''

''You're probably right.'' He reached across the table for April's free hand and playfully toyed with her slender fingers as he spoke. To his surprise, he found himself licking a drop of chocolate off her thumb. Then he said, "I'm game to run with Tom's idea. You and I can be friends in private and intellectual rivals in public. What do you say?"

April watched Sullivan as he spoke. It wasn't easy to ignore the smile that curved his mouth, the glint in his eyes, or the warmth of his lips and tongue as he licked the chocolate from her thumb. If he hadn't already made giant inroads into her sensual being, the way her hand tingled as his tongue had grazed her skin indicated he had now. Sharing a chocolate soufflé was turning out to be one of the most erotic things she'd ever done.

"All right," she said slowly.

But Lucas must have sensed her reluctance for he waved his hand dismissively. "It's only a game," he said lightly, even as his heightened emotions were proving his words false. The idea of being friends with this intriguing woman was becoming more inviting by the minute. And more dangerous to any rational thinking.

"If you want to set some rules before we start to play this game of Tom's, it's okay with me," he added. "And let's get them all out on the table now."

April looked dazed. "I'll have to let you know as we go along."

"Okay, but in spite of what you might think about me, I'm still a red-blooded guy and you're a beautiful woman. I don't want to hear any complaints about my behavior later.'' He smiled to lighten the caution.

April decided to ignore the compliment and do a little rational thinking herself. She considered Sullivan's offer. By letting her set the rules of conduct for their friendship, he was trying to be fair, and she had no problem with that. The only problem was their extreme differences on the subject of the mating game.

The idea of being friends in private warmed her middle. But sharing anything made of chocolate was going to have to be a no-no from now on.

Especially now that she was actually beginning to appreciate the softer side of Sullivan. He was everything a woman might want in a man—good looks, intelligence, humor. How he could have written ''The Mating Game'' was beyond her.

April took a deep breath. ''All right. Here's my suggestion. Let's go along with Tom. We can write a series of short and civilized articles debating 'The Mating Game.' At the same time I'll keep up the lessons. They're a good way to get to know each other better.''

Miracles do happen, Sullivan thought as he listened to April's proposal. Considering that they'd met only two days ago, time would tell what future lessons would accomplish, how their friendship would develop.

He smiled. ''Are you sure you want to go that far just to please Tom?''

April nodded. "I'm not sure I have a choice. He's my boss, after all." Besides, she thought, getting to know Sullivan might turn out to be fun, not to mention a way to put the sting of being left at the altar behind her.

Maybe it would even help to get her mother, if she believed her daughter was dating again, to stop bugging her about getting married and producing grandchildren before it was too late.

"I'll try to get Tom to hold off on publication to give us time to work on the groundwork of the debates," she said happily. "What do you think?"

Lucas reached for both her hands. He entwined his fingers with hers and squeezed them lightly. "I like your idea so much, April Morgan, that I'm willing to get started right now. How about you?"

The warmth in his eyes looked so sincere that April felt a pleasant shiver run up her spine. "Let's not get carried away, Sullivan," she said with a smile. "If we want to do this right, we'll have to take it in small steps. After all, we only just met a couple of days ago."

Lucas nodded. "Sounds wise. Only, don't let Tom wait too long to publish 'The Mating Game.' I have to have some evidence of being published before the new tenure contracts are announced."

"Got it. I'll talk to him today. In fact, he's probably downstairs at work right now. You probably know that Tom's the champion of workaholics."

"I've reconnected with Tom only recently. He still has no wife and kids waiting for him?"

"Nope. Just his father. From what I understand, Tom spends most of his time trying to prove to his father that he's as good, or better, an editor in chief and publisher as his father was."

"That makes two of us," Lucas said, his grin vanishing. "I guess it's a burden many sons of successful fathers carry." A noted sociologist, his father had expected Lucas to carry on the family tradition. And Lucas had done exactly that. With the exception of his band, research had become his life.

"Women have their burdens, too, Lucas, even me," April said ruefully. "My mother's been nagging me for ages to marry and produce grandchildren for her. That's part of what I've been trying to tell you. It might be for different reasons, but men and women have more in common than you think."

Lucas sensed he was back to treading in dangerous waters. "Let's return to the subject of our getting to know each other better. What's my next lesson?"

"I don't know," she said honestly. "How about coming to my apartment tonight for dinner and we'll talk?"

Food had been a good way to get them talking so far, Sullivan thought, so dinner tonight should be just the ticket for them to work on this friendship thing.

"Sure," he agreed. "And the deal is, friends in private, intellectual rivals in public, right?"

She nodded. "Right."

Chapter Eight

No sooner had the elevator reached Riverview's underground parking lot and they exited than April's cell phone rang again.

''Aren't you going to answer that?'' Lucas inquired when April pointedly ignored the ring.

''No, I'm not. It's probably Tom again, set on reminding me to start working on the debates,'' April answered with a scowl. ''He isn't the type to give up easily.'' Her chocolate-induced euphoria faded at the reminder that trouble could always be just a phone call away.

''What if the caller isn't Tom?''

April stopped in midstride. The only people who had her private cell phone number were her mother, Tom Eldridge, Rita and Lili. With her mother away visiting April's oldest brother, Mitchell, in Florida and providing the caller wasn't Tom, that left Rita or Lili. ''Maybe you're right,'' she said reluctantly as she lifted the small phone out of her purse, flipped it open and held it to her ear. ''April here.''

She listened for a moment. ''Sure. No, it's no problem, Lili.'' As she spoke, April handed her car keys to Sullivan and motioned to him to go ahead and click the car door open. ''Whatever I had planned for tonight can wait until tomorrow. No, honestly, I'm sure. No, it's no problem. Yes, I know you're in the emergency room at Chicago General. Try to relax and don't worry. We'll be right over.''

April folded the cell phone and dropped it in her purse. ''Something's just come up with Lili and her little boy, Paul.''

''I heard. What happened to him?'' Lucas took the keys without further comment. He knew that whatever had happened to the boy, it had to be serious, or April would never have handed over the keys without an argument.

''Would you believe Paul fell downstairs chasing his sister when they were leaving the dentist's office!'' April said as she slid into the passenger side of the car. ''Lili said he may have broken his arm. They're at the hospital right now.''

Lucas murmured his sympathy. ''Did that once myself in grade school. The kid's lucky to have his mother with him. At the time I broke mine, my mother was off somewhere 'finding' herself. I didn't get much sympathy from my father.''

April saw Lucas's lips set in a hard line. Without a loving, attentive mother in his life, no wonder he had such a poor opinion of women. ''That must have been hard on you.''

"It was, although having my classmates autograph the cast made me feel like a hero." He smiled at the long-ago memory. "How old is the kid, anyway?"

"He and his twin sister, Paulette, just turned six. Paul is like a miniature tornado and takes advantage of her. I suppose most little girls have that problem with boys until they grow up and expect equal treatment." She glanced at Sullivan. "Judging from your article, I gather you didn't know that."

Lucas's eyebrows rose. "Back to the mating-game article, are we? I thought we were talking about a six-year-old."

April grinned. "How could I forget? But you're right. I promised we'd take Paulette home and wait there with her until Lili gets home, which might not be till this evening, considering how busy emergency rooms are. Paulette is a sweet little six-year-old. Baby-sitting her will be a piece of cake."

April made sure her seat belt was fastened, Suddenly she stared at Lucas. "Good grief! I was so anxious to help I clean forgot I invited you for dinner tonight! We'll have to do it tomorrow night."

"No problem. The rain check is fine," Lucas said as he drove out of the underground parking lot and into the afternoon sunshine. His anticipation of seeing April again tomorrow night dimmed when he suddenly realized he had a more immediate problem than eating dinner alone tonight. April had used the plural when she offered to pick up Paulette! "By the way, who's the other half of the 'we'?"

"You, as in you and me." April said, looking surprised at the question. "Since Lili doesn't have any family in this country to help out when the going gets rough, it's the least I can do to take Paulette home and keep an eye on her. Otherwise she'd have to hang around an emergency room, which is no place for a little girl. You don't mind coming along and helping, do you?"

Lucas breathed a sigh of relief. Maybe baby-sitting a six-year-old girl wouldn't be all that difficult. At least no baby bottles and diapers were involved.

"No, although I *was* looking forward to having dinner with you tonight," he said with a sidelong glance at April. "Just you and me getting to know each other." He knew April's thoughts were elsewhere when she ignored him. He began to wonder if the exercise in baby-sitting would turn out to be another one of April's lessons.

He took a deep breath and started over again. "I think I should tell you that while I'm game to help out in this baby-sitting session, I do have a few reservations."

April regarded him wearily. "What kind of reservations?"

"Only that this will be a first for me. I don't know how much help I can be. I've had even less experience with small children than I had with playing baseball."

"Not to worry. If that's your only problem, I can

teach what you need to know. I'm sure we'll be able to handle it.''

''You, maybe,'' he said, as visions of what it might take to entertain a frightened little girl flashed through his mind. ''What would *I* have to do?''

To his relief, April laughed. ''Not much. Paulette doesn't need much attention. We'll just have to find a way to keep her occupied so she won't worry about her brother.''

Lucas nodded knowingly. It was beginning to look as if tonight *was* going to be another of April's lessons, after all. The first lesson had found him on a river cruise where almost all of his fellow passengers appeared to be lovers. Lesson two had ended at a baseball game with April being ejected for arguing with Tom Eldridge. After those two experiences, he shouldn't be surprised at any new ideas for lessons she came up with.

Not that he needed lessons in living in April's version of a real world. He'd managed for thirty-two years never doubting himself.

Then again, he thought ruefully as he wove through the busy Saturday-afternoon traffic, maybe that was what April meant when she'd said she intended to humanize him, or, as she'd put it, bring him into the twenty-first century. She wasn't all wrong. He knew that only a fool would think he knew more about life than anyone else.

What he was still sure of was that in trying to

make him see the real world from a twenty-first-century female viewpoint, April was playing it one lesson at a time. In other words, flying by the seat of her adorable pedal pushers.

Although he decided not to think about his skills, or rather, lack of skills, as a baby-sitter, Lucas still wondered what one did to entertain a six-year-old child, and a girl at that.

During the fifteen minutes it took him to drive to Chicago General, Lucas remembered how he'd lost his own mother when he'd been only two years older than Paulette. First to a divorce, and then some time afterward, to a fatal accident. If, all these years later, he couldn't get over that lingering feeling of loneliness and being unwanted, how could he help a little girl? And one also frightened for her twin brother?

He dropped April at the emergency-room entrance of Chicago General before finding a place to park. He marveled as April disappeared into the building. She was a generous and caring woman with more true grit in her petite frame than anyone he'd ever known, man or woman. Determined, too. Apparently nothing stopped her from trying to accomplish whatever she set her mind to, which seemed to include pursuing her present crusade to humanize him.

Instead of being disturbed at their intellectual differences and April's opinion of him, he was actually beginning to enjoy the challenge of dueling with her quick mind. She always seemed to be one step ahead of him.

Which brought him to the wisdom of agreeing to tangle with April in a series of fiery debates about the mating game. He may have received his doctorate in sociology, but it was beginning to look as if April might know more about the more practical side of life than he did.

After he parked and headed into the emergency-room waiting area, he paused at a sign pointing to the hospital gift shop. Sure that there would be too much going on in ER for anyone to miss him for a few minutes, he headed in that direction. If they were going to entertain a small frightened child, by God, they would need all the help they could get.

Ten minutes later, carrying a shopping bag filled with magazines and gift-wrapped packages, Lucas entered the ER waiting room.

"Oh, good, there you are!" April cut a swath through a swarm of doctors and nurses, patients in wheelchairs or leaning on crutches, and anxious relatives to get to him. The sound of crying children and soothing adult voices filled the air. He prayed that the sounds didn't include Paulette or her mother.

"I was afraid you'd changed your mind about helping out," April said as she led him to a curtained cubicle. "To tell the truth, I wouldn't have blamed you if you had. I'd just about decided I'd asked too much of you when I saw you coming down the hall."

"Never," he said, warming to her welcome, the gratitude that shone in her eyes, and grateful that for this time at least, April approved of him. "All you ever have to do is ask.'' He put his arm around her shoulders and hugged her. ''I'm sorry I kept you waiting. I stopped to pick up a few things I thought would keep Paulette too occupied to miss her mother and worry about her brother.''

''Great!'' April leaned into Sullivan's side and smiled up into his eyes, feeling happier than she had been for a while, despite the troubling circumstances. ''I was sure that when the chips were down, I could count on you.''

''Always.'' Lucas basked in her smile of approval. For sure, there was no chance he'd ever be able to think of April only as his editor or his teacher again. Dressed in her baseball outfit, she was all woman from the top of her silken hair to the toes of her white sneakers—loving, caring, nurturing. The first woman who actually appeared to care about him, including his mother.

Even with her creative ideas, some better than others, April had somehow managed to become an important person in his life. Amazing, considering how she'd laughed at him the first time they'd met.

So much for ''Sullivan's Rules,'' he thought wryly. April was fast becoming everything a man could possibly want in a woman.

He was falling for her. Maybe even too much to enter into a series of no-hold-barred debates that might strain their tenuous relationship.

He didn't care what Tom might think of him if he refused to debate April. He and Tom had set out on different paths in college, and it wouldn't be a big surprise to find out they had a few differences fifteen years later.

The only problem with his backing out now was that April might think he doubted his own research methods or his conclusions. He didn't. Although, after hanging around April the past couple of days, he was beginning to think there might be more to the mating game than his research revealed.

There was April's smile, he reflected as he thought of her. Her warm and generous heart, her quick mind and a body that made him ache to hold—preferably while he made love to her.

"So, what do you have in the shopping bag?" April broke into his thoughts as she led him to the cubicle where Lili and Paulette were waiting while Paul was having his arm X-rayed. Paulette was huddled in a chair beside her mother.

"You'll just have to wait and see," Lucas said as he tried to force his thoughts away from making love to April. There was something more important going on here, a forlorn-looking little girl. He sauntered over to Paulette and handed her the colorful shopping bag. "Hi. I'm Lucas Sullivan, a friend of April's." When she looked over at her mother, he smiled gently. "I was told that since half the fun of receiving gifts is unwrapping them, I had everything gift-wrapped for you to open. How about it?"

"For a guy who said he doesn't know squat about little kids, you manage to do okay, Sullivan," April said as she came up behind him. "Paulette will love unwrapping them, won't you, sweetheart?"

Lucas felt as if he'd finally received April's seal of approval. Even his considerable academic achievements and the ceremony where he'd received his doctorate hadn't made him feel so proud of himself. And all because he'd bought a few gifts to please a little girl.

Paulette took the shopping bag with a smile that lit up her piquant face. He glimpsed a row of tiny white teeth with one missing in the middle. He'd never dreamed that the approval of one small child would make him feel like a man.

Maybe April had been right. Maybe he needed a family of his own in order to see the real world.

A doctor entered the cubicle with Paul. "I'm afraid there's a break in the arm, all right. Although, I'm happy to tell you, it's a clean one." He gave little Paul a reassuring smile. "We'll have you in a cast in a few minutes, young man." He motioned to the purple bruise on Paul's forehead. "I'd like to keep him here awhile longer, make sure he doesn't have a concussion."

"Of course," Lili said. She turned to April. "So are you sure you don't mind taking Paulette home and waiting there with her until Paul and I get home?"

Paulette started to wail. "I don't want to go home without you, Mommy! I want to say here with you and Paul!"

Lili gathered her daughter in her arms and hugged her. ''Don't cry, baby. We don't know how long it will be before your brother can go home. You'll be much better off at home with Auntie April and Mr. Sullivan to take care of you.''

''No!'' Paulette's sobbing increased.

Lucas bent over her. ''Don't you want to open all the nice presents I bought you?'' Paulette shook her head. ''It'll be just like Christmas morning.''

Paulette's tears slowed to a hiccup. Her eyes fastened on the brightly wrapped package Lucas held out to her, then she nodded shyly. ''Okay.''

Two hours later, with Lili and Paul still at Chicago General, Paulette sat enthroned on a pillow in the living room in April's apartment. In spite of her assurances that Paulette's mother would be home soon, the girl's lips still quivered.

Lucas's heart went out to her. He'd learned from Lili at the hospital that she and her brother had been playing hide-and-seek when he'd tripped and fallen down the stairs. She no doubt felt that she'd been the cause of her brother's accident.

He knew the feeling.

In his case, his parents' quarrel and subsequent divorce might have had nothing to do with him, but at only eight and too young to understand the problem between his parents, he still remembered feeling he was somehow to blame.

He dropped to the floor beside Paulette just as April came into the room carrying a glass of milk and a plate of cookies, which she set on the coffee table beside Paulette.

''Hey, how about a glass of milk for me, too?'' Lucas asked, looking wistfully at the chocolate-chip cookies. Treats like that had been entirely absent in his upbringing after his mother left. His father, firm in his belief that cookies, even just an occasional one, were bad for a growing boy, had insisted on fresh fruit, instead. A habit Lucas had generally pursued, but with an occasional act of defiance.

''Paulette, I'm really hungry. How about sharing some of those cookies with me?''

April smothered a laugh when Paulette shyly looked to her for approval. ''Go ahead, baby. Give Mr. Sullivan as many as he wants. There's more in the cookie jar. It's the least we can do, since he's being so nice to us, right?''

Paulette nodded. ''Okay, since you're being so nice,'' she echoed, and handed Lucas a cookie.

''How about opening a present?'' Lucas coaxed when April disappeared into the kitchen area to prepare something for dinner. While he watched, she placed a container of frozen macaroni and cheese in the microwave to thaw. ''You'll feel a lot better as soon as you do, I promise.''

Paulette reached into the shopping bag, drew out a square box, unwrapped it and stared at the cover. ''It looks like a chemistry set!''

April came back into the room and broke into laughter. ''Okay, Sullivan, now I believe you,'' she said. "You don't know anything about little girls, or big ones, either."

Lucas didn't appreciate the latter part of the sentence. He suspected April was talking about herself, but he wasn't prepared to launch into a defense at the moment. Not with an audience. Eventually though, he wanted to tell her that big girls and the way their minds worked was a subject in which he considered himself an expert. He glanced at Paulette. "What's wrong with a chemistry set? I had one when I was a kid. You can make all kinds of things with it. Look, even pretty crystals."

April's conscience kicked in. Even if Sullivan's choice for a little girl's entertainment was a bit unusual, his heart was in right place.

"What are the other gifts?" She glanced at Paulette, who seemed actually quite absorbed in checking out the contents of the chemistry set. "I hope it's not a gun and a holster," she added in a whisper.

He looked shocked. "Of course not! I'm not an idiot."

April was tempted to tell Sullivan that indeed he was not. Rather, he was a man with a big heart. He seemed to have changed overnight.

She also would have liked to show him how the change in him was affecting her. To give way to the need she felt to be in his arms, to have him hold her close. It was too bad that Paulette had ended her perusal of the chemistry set and was now eagerly anticipating another present, or she would have.

The next gift turned out to be a Spider-Man figure complete with a set of comic books covering the figure's exploits!

This time, April kept a straight face. But Paulette surprised her.

"Oh!" the little girl exclaimed, holding Spider-Man up. "You got something for my brother when he comes home. He *loves* Spider-Man! Then she reached for the next package and unwrapped it.

It was a miniature wooden train set, complete with railroad tracks and train station, including tiny figures of passengers.

Paulette beamed. "Wow. Now I have a train just like Paul," she said happily. "We don't have to fight over who gets to play with it anymore."

Lucas felt like a hero when Paulette dropped the box and jumped into his arms. "Thank you, thank you, thank you," she said smacking a kiss on his cheek.

As for April, she simply watched the scene with her mouth agape. When she bestowed one of her beautiful smiles on him, Lucas thought it was beginning to look as if he'd finally done something right.

Chapter Nine

Torn by mixed emotions, the following evening Sullivan found himself more than ready to cash in his rain check.

He was standing in front of the door to April's apartment, waiting for her to answer his knock. He didn't know how April actually felt about him now that their shared baby-sitting duty was over, but he had a feeling their relationship had undergone a major shift. What had started out as a mutual education on the subject of what went into the mating game had definitely changed yesterday.

He'd seen a new tenderness in April's eyes as she sat on the floor watching him assemble miniature wooden tracks and trains and playing train conductor with Paulette. Even his pleasure at the chocolate-chip cookies and cold glass of milk seemed to have earned him some Brownie points.

And both those experiences had been such simple pleasures, he thought. Pleasures a man should have enjoyed as a child or as a father.

In retrospect, he couldn't remember a woman ever looking at him the way April had looked at him. Not a female acquaintance and certainly not his mother. Whatever the reason for her tender smile, April had made him feel ten feet tall.

Almost overnight, he'd come to realize their relationship, at least on his part, hadn't remained all business. He'd fallen for April.

He listened for her footsteps on the other side of the door. When he heard them, they sounded even, sure, which meant he couldn't use a twisted ankle as an excuse to pick her up in his arms, but he didn't intend to give up. He'd find a way to have her in his arms again, or he wasn't the man he thought he was.

The door was flung open. "Hi," April said brightly. "You're late. I was afraid you'd come down with a case of cold feet!"

It was too true. He'd had a few misgivings about showing April he cared for her, but he felt encouraged by her welcoming smile. "Sorry, I'm still without wheels. I finally caught a cab, but I wasn't the only one who wanted one."

April was more breathtaking tonight than ever, he thought as they stood in the doorway trading smiles. The businesslike office persona and the sporty persona wearing pedal pushers of the past few days were gone. Tonight she was dressed in a long flowered dress with a plunging neckline that made it clear she wasn't wearing a bra. A simple gold chain hung around her elegant neck to nestle in the valley between her breasts. Gold earrings dangled from her ears. On her feet, she wore strappy sandals that matched her red-painted toes. The only incongruous element was the frilly white apron around her waist.

With her hair hanging loose around her shoulders and the gold earrings swinging as she spoke, April took his breath away. She was a bewildering mixture of sensuality and domesticity.

He wondered what she was up to. If it was another lesson, he was ready, willing and able.

Still, he found himself concentrating on her lips, her straight white teeth, and wondering if it was too soon to kiss her the way he wanted to.

Until he remembered that in spite of the apron she wore tonight, the April Morgan he'd met a few days ago had been determined to show him she was the last woman to fit the role of a woman out to please her man. And, he reminded himself, he was here tonight to discuss a series of no-holds-barred debates on the subject of the mating game, not for a seduction.

Except…it was impossible not to think sensual thoughts with April looking at him as if he were a chocolate soufflé.

Which part was she playing tonight? The cool, pragmatic editor or the sexy woman smiling at him in the doorway?

"Come in," she said. "Dinner's almost ready."

He took a deep breath and trailed her into the apartment where a small dining-room table was set for two with shining crystal glasses, fine china and gleaming cutlery. In the center of the table was a bowl of white daisies, flanked by two tall red candles.

The scent of spices filled the air. Soft music played in the background.

Something more than met the eye was going on here, he thought. Whatever it was, he intended to enjoy every moment.

"How are Lili and the kids doing?" he asked. He'd followed her into the kitchen.

"Great," April answered from where she was bent over the oven. "Lili sends her thanks. She also said Spider-Man and the comic books are keeping Paul occupied. Paulette wants to know when you're going to come over to play train again."

For a moment, Lucas lost his voice. Baby-sitting yesterday afternoon and evening—Lili and Paul had arrived about eight—had been a first. A six-year-old girl expecting him to show up for play was another. Right now, he wanted to concentrate on a *big* girl. April.

"The kid liked me enough to want *me* to come over and play with her?"

April turned around, wooden spoon in one hand, a towel in the other. "Why are you so surprised? You shouldn't be. I'm not the only one who's discovered that under that academic exterior of yours beats a human heart."

Lucas felt embarrassed when she added with a soft

smile, "I first suspected the truth about you when you took me for the chocolate soufflé. After watching the way you played with Paulette, I was certain of it."

Lucas felt bewildered but amused. Having bypassed a normal childhood himself, who'd have thought he'd actually *enjoy* playing trains with Paulette last night?

More important, just as his love of music had turned his life around, his newfound ability to relate to children, and they to him, was another turning point.

He wasn't the only person to undergo a metamorphosis, he thought as he looked around the homey apartment. April, the no-nonsense magazine editor set on reforming him and showing him the real world women lived and worked in, had apparently changed along with him and turned into a veritable temptress. And all because he'd been a success at baby-sitting?

He wasn't going to ask.

"Well, don't just stand there, Sullivan, what do you think?" She gestured at the dining-room table, which could be seen from the kitchen. "Surprise number one," she said with an impish grin. "A special dinner for you."

"No lessons tonight?"

"Wait and see," April said with a smile. Dimples danced across her cheeks.

Sullivan had an idea that tonight was going to be full of surprises. Considering the welcome change in

April, he intended to do his share to contribute to whatever she had in mind.

April turned back to the oven before Sullivan could notice the look on her face. He was getting too good at reading her. Tonight he was in for a surprise, and it wasn't just that tonight would have to double as lesson number four, since yesterday's baby-sitting session had unexpectedly turned into a lesson on the importance of children in a relationship. Tonight's lesson was designed to show Sullivan that when it came to pragmatic reasons for a male-female attraction, his mind-over-matter theory wasn't worth a plugged nickel.

As for the more popular theory that the mating game was an instinctive search for strong genes and Rita's theory that the mating game was based on sexual attraction, both seemed valid, for they were inextricably linked; the former created the latter.

When she looked at Sullivan, dressed in a casual brown jacket, matching Dockers, a beige shirt and brown tie, she saw a handsome man, obviously healthy and strong. He *had* to have strong genes.

And she was very sexually attracted to him.

If only Rita's claim that sex was the answer to the mating game was as simple as it sounded, she mused as she gazed at Sullivan, she would have managed to separate him from his alter ego. At least in her mind.

April shook off her thoughts. "How about making

yourself at home while I put the finishing touches to dinner?''

Sullivan left the kitchen and returned only moments later. He'd taken off his jacket and tie; his shirt sleeves were rolled up above his elbows, and the top two buttons of his shirt were unbuttoned. She caught a glimpse of curly brown hair on his chest.

If this was how he made himself at home, she was in trouble.

''Anything I can do for you?'' He helped himself to a carrot slice from a bowl of raw vegetables.

''Sure.'' She handed him a salad bowl. ''The romaine is washed and drained. All you have to do is tear it into bite-size pieces, then add the cut-up vegetables. The dressing and a bottle of wine are in the refrigerator.''

''Got it!'' He went to work.

As Sullivan's long fingers wrestled with the romaine leaves, she closed her eyes and imagined those fingers stroking her bare skin.

''Something get in your eye?'' Sullivan moved closer and gently pushed her hair aside. ''Here, open wide while I take a look.''

April blinked and stepped out of his reach. ''Whatever was in there seems to be gone now, thanks.''

The last thing she wanted was Sullivan's eyes gazing into hers. Only a fool wouldn't have known how she felt about him. She might think he was naive when it came to the mating game, but she'd already learned that both he and his alter ego were far from being fools.

"I'm fine, really. I was just trying to think if I've remembered everything, *Dr.* Sullivan. I'll let you know if I need any more medical assistance."

He raised an eyebrow. "Anytime, Ms. Morgan. Just say the word. I actually know how to fix a lot of things besides sprained ankles."

The memory of his hands on her ankle and foot almost made her blush. She turned away. "What you can do now is take the salad dressing and wine out of the refrigerator. And then you can add the dressing to the salad and toss."

Sullivan chuckled. "I can, huh? Whatever you say, ma'am."

April pulled on her oven mitts and drew out the roasting pan filled with the lamb-and-fresh-vegetable kabobs. "Here, come smell this. I love the aroma of spices, don't you?"

When she bent over the pan, Sullivan followed her lead, inhaling the rich spices, distracted by her faint lemony scent and the flushed cheek inches from his.

Too aware of Sullivan's close proximity, April straightened and moved away, transferred the steaming skewers to a serving plate, filled a bowl with rice and put them on a serving tray.

"Put this on the table, would you please," she said briskly. "Let's eat before everything cools down."

She took off her apron, picked up the salad bowl and took it to the table. The romantic music she'd intended to create the proper atmosphere for the lesson that the attraction between sexes was based on more than a simple set of rules was still playing. It had more than done its job, and not only on Sullivan.

Lucas waited until April was seated and had shaken out her napkin. "Everything on the table looks great. So why do I get the feeling that you're bursting to tell me something? Here, maybe this will help loosen your tongue." He uncorked the wine and reached over to fill her glass, then poured one for himself.

Darn, April thought. She'd wanted to save her little surprise till *after* they'd eaten. But then again, what was the point? Her news wasn't going to be any better an hour from now. She took a sip of her wine and considered how to tell him.

"I'm afraid I have some bad news for you," she began.

Sullivan paused as he reached for the salad bowl. So he'd been right about something bothering April. "Can't it wait until after dinner?"

"There's no use waiting," she said and put her napkin on the table.

Sullivan wanted to point out that he hadn't derailed her interest in her chocolate soufflé at lunch yesterday by talking about Tom's disturbing cellphone call. He didn't want any bad news to disrupt the intimate atmosphere tonight. If April had plans for them, so did he.

"Uh-oh," he said with a grin. "I have a feeling I'm about to get a good news/bad news sandwich."

She looked startled at the metaphor. "What kind of sandwich?"

"You know," he said, seemingly unconcerned with her reaction. "One of those 'first say something nice, then a sock it to 'em filling before you close with a nice observation.' Am I right?"

He was more right than he knew, April thought as she nodded slowly. "I spoke to Tom this afternoon about holding off the publication date of your article so that we'd have time to work on the groundwork of the debates."

"And?"

She took a deep breath. "Tom thinks your article is too good to keep. He's pulled back the feature article in the August issue and substituted yours. Even changed the cover of the issue. To help sales, he said."

"That's supposed to be the bad news part of the sandwich? As long as he hasn't made any changes to the article, I couldn't care less."

"No, of course not. He told me to quit trying to make any suggestions for changes."

"So what's the bad news?"

"He wants us to get started on that series of cutting-edge debates right away, so that they're ready for the *next* issue."

He gazed at her over the rim of his wineglass. The flickering candlelight revealed a humorous glint in his eyes. ''We don't have to start tonight, I hope.'' Even though he'd come tonight expecting they would, he felt quite differently now.

April felt a tingling run through her body from the top of her head to her toes. ''Well...we do have to get started really soon.''

''Not tonight,'' he repeated. ''Anything else? If so, you may as well spit it out now.''

''No, not really. I'm just glad you're not upset about starting work on the debates right away.''

Lucas dismissed April's version of bad news. As far as he was concerned, Tom had already accomplished what he'd suspected Tom wanted to do—arranged events to boost circulation. And unless he'd missed his guess, to get him and April together. The rest was up to him.

April bit her lower lip. She might have been initially annoyed, or even dismayed by Sullivan's ridiculous approach to the mating game, but now she was no longer troubled by what he thought. She was actually beginning to *care* for the man in ways that had nothing to do with his academic side, and she wasn't certain that a public conflict and private friendship, or more, could coexist.

''So *is* it okay if we pass on working on the debates tonight?'' Sullivan asked as he folded his napkin and pushed away from the table.

April nodded hesitantly. She'd intended to surprise him, but it looked as if he was about to surprise her.

Sullivan paused and studied her for a long moment. Reading her mind again, "How about lessons three and four? Can those wait for another time, too?"

"Truthfully," she confessed, determined to taste the passion she sensed in Sullivan and was growing inside her, "not that I planned it this way, but lesson three was last night at Lili's when we baby-sat Paulette."

"That was the feeling I had," he said as he got to his feet, "but I wasn't certain. I take it I did well?"

April blushed. In planning to teach him lesson number four tonight, she'd also learned something about herself. That even without the excuse of her injured ankle, she wanted Sullivan's arms around her. And not to help her, but to make love to her.

Rita would have been proud of her!

"Whatever you have in mind for lesson four, let's do it some other time," Sullivan said after another long and thoughtful look at her. He walked around the table and held out his hand. "I have a better idea about what to do with the rest of the evening than talking about debates. How about you?"

She couldn't bring herself to tell him lesson four had begun the moment he'd stepped in the door. A lesson intended to demonstrate that when confronted with a woman he finds desirable, a man's rational mind turns to mush. If he hadn't believed it before, it certainly looked as if he believed it now.

Mesmerized by the warm look in Sullivan's eyes, April gave him her hand, rose to her feet and, before she could stop to wonder why, moved into his arms. "I can't believe this is really you, Sullivan," she said as she rubbed her cheek against his chest and inhaled the scent of wine on his lips.

"Forget Sullivan," he murmured. "Let's pretend I left him at the front door." He bent to kiss the side of her mouth. "This is me, Lucas, holding you. Can't you tell? If not, I'm willing to show you."

April smiled up at him as his eyes searched hers and his fingers gently outlined her lips. Impulsively, she took one finger and kissed it before she let it go. "I wasn't sure. In fact," she said with a laugh, "I've never been really sure there are two sides of you, although I suspected it a couple of times."

"Oh? When?"

She couldn't bring herself to tell him about seeing him perform at the Roxy nightclub. Or that his sensual performance had lit her fire the moment he'd danced on stage. "Last night with little Paulette, for one."

"Anything else?" he asked as his fingers toyed with the neckline of her gown.

April's senses sang as his fingers brushed her skin. "Isn't the fact that I think you've changed enough?"

"If I've changed, it's only because I'd never met anyone like you before," he said as he bent to kiss the nape of her neck. Gently, at first, then with an intensity that surprised her.

"Have I told you I've become a recent convert to your friend Rita's theory?" he said into her silence.

He bent and kissed her breasts, first one, then the other.

"No, but it's never too late," April replied when she was able to think again. She stroked his bent head, loving the feel of his hair under her fingers. Thrilled by the sensation of his lips against her skin. "Tell me, Doctor, does your expertise in the art of healing extend to dealing with a rapid heartbeat?"

"Do I need to write a prescription?" he murmured. "If so, I'll be happy to oblige."

"No," she whispered. "Just show me."

He laughed and clasped her to him until she had trouble breathing. "First, we forget dinner. Then I blow out the candles so the flames won't start a fire." He paused to demonstrate. "In fact," he continued as he turned down the lights, then picked her up and carried her to the sofa, "the only fire I intend to start around here is the one I hope to kindle in you."

"Is there a fire in you, too, Sullivan?" she whispered, although she felt his arousal against her middle. She didn't need to ask.

"Give me a minute and I'll show you." He sank onto the couch with her in his arms. "There's a fire that started the moment you opened the door and I got a good look at you."

April blushed as she remembered her own physical reaction when she'd opened the door to him.

"Tonight *was* intended to be another lesson, wasn't it," he added as he kissed the nape of her neck.

''Lucky guess,'' she gasped when he bent his head and kissed her breasts again.

''Even stuffy professors are known to behave like red-blooded men given the right time, the right place and the right woman,'' he said softly as he pulled the gown down off her shoulders.

''So, how does a man makes love to a red-blooded woman?'' April asked breathlessly. Even in the dim light that still surrounded them, she could see the glow in his eyes deepen.

He paused to take off his shirt. ''For starters, like this.'' He cradled her face between two hands and brushed her lips with his. ''The truth is, I've actually been thinking warm thoughts about you ever since lesson one on the river cruise, April Morgan,'' he said, pausing to gaze deeply into her eyes. ''I guess there was always another side of me just waiting to do what comes naturally. Like now,'' he said as he bent over her, ''and only because it's you.''

''Are you sure?'' April asked, and stilled the lips that sought her other breast. ''I was only trying to show you tonight that given the right time, the right place and the right stimulus, the human heart will rule the most academic mind.'' She gasped when he blew gently in her ear.

''You did a damn good job. You're one hell of a stimulus,'' he murmured, erasing any doubt she might have had with his warm lips. ''Now, stop thinking so much, sweetheart. Let yourself go and just *feel,* while I show you how I feel about you.''

He feathered her face, the nape of her neck and her bared breasts with kisses.

The taste of him, the feel of strong, muscular arms holding her and the deep and sensuous timbre in his voice as he whispered in her ear drove her to distraction. The tenderness she saw in his eyes melted her heart.

She was more than ready to let him take her to a place where only a man who saw her as a real woman could take her.

He ran his hands over her aching breasts and to her waist, then smiled. "You have entirely too many clothes on for what I have in mind for dessert, April love," he said softly.

"Dessert? We haven't had the main course yet," she said with a shaky laugh.

"Maybe this *is* the main course," he replied.

April sighed. "You're right, dinner can wait." She raised her arms. "I could use a little help here."

"My pleasure." With one swift movement, he bunched the hem of her gown in his hands, then drew it up and off her with a flourish. Then he hooked a finger in her thong and she obligingly lifted her hips. When he'd divested her of the last barrier between them, he looked at her, and said, "you're so beautiful you'd take my breath away if I didn't need it to show you how I feel about you."

She lay in his arms, her body on fire while he paid attention to her breasts. "Feel good?" he whispered.

"Very good," April whispered in return. "Don't stop now."

He laughed, then began to feather kisses down her body to her waist while his hands pleasured her. "More?"

"Yes, and only with you," she agreed softly as she reached to run her hands over his bare shoulders where a fine sheen was forming. "You still have too many clothes on for what *I* have in mind," she said deliberately echoing his words.

He grinned and opened his arms. "I was just waiting to make sure this is what you really wanted. Go ahead. I'm all yours."

April gestured to his slacks. He shucked them. "I think you're beautiful, too," she said admiringly when he was completely nude, and magnificent in his manhood.

"I'm glad you think so," he said wryly. "I wouldn't want to disappoint." He took her in his arms again.

"You don't," she managed to say before his lips took hers. "The couch or the bed?"

"The bed, this time," he muttered. "The couch later." He picked her up and carried her into the bedroom. "I need an ample playing field for what I have in mind for this game of ours. All you need to do is decide on the rules like you promised."

Game? April thought fleetingly. This was no game, not to her. Her heart ached at the thought of this being a game to him.

"I've decided that only fools make rules at a time like this," she said.

"Right! I promised to show you how to cure a rapid heartbeat and I intend to deliver!" He bent over the bed, swept back the covers and lowered her to the mattress. Instead of joining her, he paused and ran his fingers through his tousled hair. "Damn!" he said. "Give me a minute, sweetheart. I'll be right back."

Her body a heated pool of longing, April lay there waiting while he strode out of the bedroom. Seconds later, he was back. He'd remembered to protect her.

April gave herself up to his arms while he made them one. Kiss by kiss, stroke by stroke, her heartfelt little sighs joined by his, she matched his movements until she tumbled into another world and bursts of pleasure shot through her.

She held on to Lucas until she heard his shout of pleasure. Together, they'd gone to a magical place where only he could have taken her.

Her heart full, she cuddled, spoon fashion, into his arms. If it was going to be for only one night, at least for tonight he was hers.

Chapter Ten

The pressure of an arm thrown across her waist awoke April from an erotic dream in which Sullivan was making passionate love to her again. Reluctant to awake and let the dream go, she slowly turned her head and opened her eyes.

He lay on his stomach, his head resting near her bare shoulder, his lips a breath away from hers. The arm that held her so possessively to him was his.

He'd been as good as his promise, April thought with a delicious shiver. First, they'd made love in the king-size bed, fiercely, as if they couldn't get enough of each other. When they'd satisfied their first hunger, there'd been a hurried snack of cold lamb-and-vegetable kabobs at midnight to satisfy another kind of hunger.

The narrow couch had come next. He always kept his promises, Sullivan had told her with a solemn face when she'd protested there wasn't room there for two. He'd been right. She'd quickly discovered they hadn't needed a king-size bed to make the uninhibited yet tender kind of love again she'd yearned for.

He'd laughingly told her the night was still young and carried her back to bed. He'd turned out to be right. She dimly remembered falling asleep cuddled in his arms.

She sank back against the pillows and studied Sullivan as he slept. Long brown lashes lay across his cheeks. A hint of musk, a reminder of their lovemaking, clung to him. The scent of the chocolate latte she made for him during their midnight raid on the kitchen lingered on his breath.

Erotic visions of hot, slick skin sliding across her hot skin, tangled limbs and rumpled sheets sent new waves of warmth racing through her. Playful, tender kisses that had turned passionate and whispered words of endearment still flooded her senses.

He'd even sung a song he'd written shortly before they'd met, "Coming Home to Love." He'd laughingly told her he must have known they would meet and that the song was meant for her.

She glanced at the clock beside the bed. It was almost dawn. If Sullivan-turned-Lucas had any more promises he intended to keep, she thought with a shiver, the time was now.

"Thinking again?" a lazy voice said in her ear. The arm that held her pulled her closer. "I was hoping I convinced you to let that habit of yours go last night."

April laughed and leaned over him. ''Some. Actually, I was thinking of you.''

The first rays of dawn sliding through the bedroom window shutters lit up his pleased smile. ''I'm glad,'' he answered as he ran his fingers across her lips. ''You looked so serious that for a minute I was afraid you were thinking of getting out of bed to clean up the kitchen.''

Eager to taste last night's pleasures again, April put her misgivings away and nestled closer into his inviting warmth. Her hand slid down his thigh. ''What kitchen?''

He caught her hand, laughed and held it to his lips. ''Forget what I said, sweetheart. I don't know what I could have been thinking when I asked the question.'' He nipped her chin playfully and blew in her ear until her already heightened senses took wing.

''What I do know,'' he continued, ''is that we haven't played all the innings of the game we started last night. I don't know about you, but I wouldn't want the game to end too soon.''

''*Is* this a game?'' Uncomfortable at the thought that last night *had* been only a game to him, April gazed questioningly into his eyes. ''Tell me, which man are you this morning—Sullivan or Lucas?''

''Definitely not Sullivan, love.'' He brought his mouth to hers, urging hers open, tasting her again. ''I left him at the door last night, remember?''

''I remember,'' she said, reluctant to ask what he meant by the word *love.* Had it been only a casual word of endearment, the sort that came so easily to some, or did it have a deeper meaning?

Lucas sensed the uncertainty in her voice. The questioning look in her eyes that told him more than he cared to know. She was unsure of him. Something he'd said was troubling her. Damn his big mouth!

Maybe he hadn't done enough to show April that the academic Sullivan side of him existed only on the pages of his manuscript. Maybe he hadn't shown her how desirable she was, not as his editor or a teacher in the mating game, but as a woman.

"I think I need to do something more to help you remember." He playfully rubbed his nose across hers to lighten the moment. "Ready?"

To his relief, she nodded. "I am if you are."

Lucas lay back, took her hand and replaced it on his thigh.

Wordlessly, April leaned over him and smiled into his eyes while her hands slowly roamed his thighs, his firm bottom, the dark brown curls around his arousal. "Do you like this as much as I do when you do this to me?"

"Too much." He said with a groan. He flipped her over on her back, sheathed himself and entered her with one firm thrust. "I just don't want it to end too soon."

Waves of exquisite pleasure washed over April, tumbling her over and over again until she fell h[illegible] long into their depths. Deeper and deeper s[illegible] savoring every moment, afraid to think of what the day would bring. For now, she wanted only to feel.

Finally washed ashore on an ebbing tide of pleasure, April opened her eyes. "Good morning, Lucas," she said as she smiled up at him and called him by his given name for the first time since they'd been introduced four short days ago.

"And a good morning it certainly is." He rolled off her, fell to her side with a sigh. "Uh, I hate to mention it at a time like this, but what are the chances you can satisfy another kind of hunger of mine?"

April didn't think she could move, not after a bout of lovemaking that left her limp and happy. But she had to be fair. They'd skipped eating dinner last night. "A midnight snack of kabobs and a chocolate latte wasn't enough for you?"

"With an insatiable woman like you," he said, leering playfully at her, "a guy needs to keep up his strength!"

April smothered a giggle and slid out of bed. Lesson four had not only worked, it had gone beyond her wildest dreams. Unexpectedly; she'd also learned a lesson of her own: she was still vulnerable to charismatic men. She glanced back to where a smiling Lucas looked too satisfied with himself for her own good. Maybe she would be wise to play for the moment what this apparently was to him—a game. She could avoid getting hurt again.

"Give me five minutes," she called over her

shoulder as she made for the bathroom to shower and change. ''I'll have to look around and see what's left in the pantry.''

''I can hardly wait,'' he called after her and slid out of bed. He rubbed his chin where dark stubble was beginning to appear. ''Hold on a minute, I've changed my mind. First things first. How about if I joined you in the shower?''

''Now I *know* you're Lucas this morning.'' April held out her hand to him. ''An academic like Sullivan would never suggest anything as erotic as showering together. If he had, he never would have done his study.''

''The poor man only scratched the surface,'' Lucas agreed, scratching his chin. ''After tonight, I'm sure there's a second study in the works.'' With that he scooped her up in his arms, carried her into the bathroom and into the shower, where he set her on her feet. Before she had a chance to protest, he turned on the cold water.

''Oh, my!'' April shrank from the cold, brisk spray. ''That's too cold!''

Lucas adjusted the hot-water control, laughing. ''Sorry, I thought we both needed to cool off. Solemnly regarding her taut nipples, he reached for the soap, lathered it between his hands and slid his soapy hands slowly and sensuously around her breasts.

''How about now? Warmer?''

''Better.'' She raised her arms to put them around his neck.

"Not good enough," he said. He lathered the lemon-scented soap again and washed her tingling body from her shoulders to her toes. To add to her pleasure, he took care to stop at places in between.

April forgot the change in the water temperature. Who needed hot water when Lucas's touch was turning her body into an inferno? "Is this another specialty of yours?"

"It wasn't before, but it is now," he replied. "More?"

"Later," she said, eyeing his arousal. "It's my turn now."

He handed her the soap with a bow. "I'm all yours."

Lucas groaned as she slid her soapy hands over him. "I don't know if I mentioned it before," he said when she reached the most intimate part of him, "but from now on trading specialties with you is going to be another favorite pastime of mine."

April felt Lucas's arousal against her thighs and looked up into his smile—a blatant invitation to making love here in the shower if ever she'd seen one. "Here?" He nodded. She gulped. "You can't—"

"Sure I can." He took the soap out of her hand, put it back in its holder and reached for her. "Here, let me show you."

He not only demonstrated a new and tumultuous way of making love, it was beginning to look as if his hunger for food would have to wait awhile longer. She was sure Lucas wouldn't mind. Certainly she didn't.

When she was finally back in the bedroom to dress while he shaved, April mused contentedly that now was a good time to continue to mend the errors of the Sullivan side of Lucas. She liked his suggestion of a second study. Perhaps they could work on it together. Between them, they could provide enough research material. Only this time she intended to make sure his conclusions weren't based on answers to a questionnaire filled out by students anxious to please. If she had her way, the answers were going to come from two people who lived in a real world.

Rational thinking be damned.

LUCAS SIGHED AND PUSHED away his empty plate. "April, everything about you is wonderful. Even your cooking!"

April paused in midbite. The only cooking she'd done this morning consisted of opening a can of corned-beef hash she found in the pantry. "Everything?"

He caught her meaning with a grin. "Everything!"

She eyed him demurely. "Thank you."

He took a swallow of coffee and eyed her thoughtfully. "Come to think of it, you just might turn out to be the perfect woman."

"The perfect woman?" April's pleasure faded abruptly. "You mean like the type in your article?"

Lucas peered at her over the rim of his cup. "I

hadn't quite thought of you that way until now,'' he said with a smile. ''You wouldn't need a lot of changes.''

Hurt at the implication she could become the woman described in ''The Mating Game'' if she tried harder, April gathered up the empty dishes and carried them to the sink. ''Whatever you were thinking about how I might change, the answer is no. I'm not about to become a Sullivan woman. As for you, it looks as if you're back to being the same old Sullivan, after all. Maybe I read more into last night and just now in the shower than I should have. Maybe there really aren't two sides of you.''

She poured liquid soap into a sink filled with soaking dishes from last night, then added the dishes from breakfast and turned on the hot water. No dishwasher for her this morning, she fumed. She had to keep her hands busy or she'd hit him over the head with the frying pan. How could one man be so obtuse? How could he not know how much it hurt for her to be compared to the woman he espoused in his ridiculous article?

''Furthermore, as far as I'm concerned, there are no *ifs* about the mating game,'' April said, angry at herself for falling for the man she *wanted* him to be rather than the man he actually was. ''Like I said before, no sane woman would turn herself into a Stepford Wife in order to win a man. It doesn't pay off. I should know, I tried.''

''Oops!'' He came up behind her and put his arms

around her middle. "I'm sorry. I guess I really stuck my foot in it this time, didn't I."

"Both feet." She tested the water temperature. Just right.

He nuzzled her neck.

She handed him a towel.

He handed it back. "Why don't you tell me in detail exactly why you feel so strongly about my take on the mating game? From the way I can feel your heart beating, I'm beginning to suspect there's something more personal about this than what's in an editor's job description."

April turned in his arms. He was right. She *had* taken the rules in his article personally. He had to believe what he'd written or he wouldn't have said that she almost fit his idea of a perfect woman, an ideal mate. If only, she thought, Sullivan had stayed a Lucas. She had no right to be disappointed. He might have been an eager participant in her "lessons," but he'd been honest with her about not being interested in the mating game for himself. The fact that he'd called her a "Sullivan woman" was all the proof she needed.

She saw the genuine concern in his eyes. After all they'd been to each other in the past twenty-four hours, she did owe him the truth. He'd been up front with her. She had to be the same for him.

She dried her hands on the towel and threw it aside. "You're right, although I didn't realize it until now." She took a deep breath. "I once talked myself into believing my ex-fiancé loved me. It turns out I didn't know him, any more than I knew myself.''

''Don't, April,'' Sullivan said when her voice broke. ''I was out of line for asking. Whatever happened before now is none of my business.''

''It is, because it does concern you.'' She took another deep breath and went on. ''Anyway, in retrospect, I realize I'd decided it was time to get married and have a family. Fortunately, Jim eloped with one of my bridesmaids just minutes before the wedding. I see now that she's a woman who actually is the type you describe in your article. Thank goodness I finally realized that by being jilted, I'd actually gotten lucky. I wasn't ready to turn into a Sullivan woman for him, and I'm not ready to turn into one for you.''

''Just my luck,'' he said ruefully. ''that I had to remind you of him.''

''What you've done is remind me of my narrow escape,'' April said. ''I realize now I was wrong in trying to change you into the man *I* thought you should be. I should have realized you can't change a person. People can only change themselves.''

''Then this isn't about feeling sorry about last night or this morning, I hope?''

''No. It's my fault for letting our relationship get this far,'' April said, willing herself not to throw herself into his arms. ''This time with you has been wonderful. What I am sorry about is that I had no right to expect you to change for me.''

''You're not all wrong,'' Lucas said as he held her by her upper arms when she tried to break away and kissed her lightly on the forehead. ''I guess I had something I had to prove, too. You might think my study and the article Tom asked me to write are off the mark, but actually they're not. You might not think so, but I do know all women aren't alike. It's just that some are more suited for marriage than others. I honestly believe the study and the article I wrote for Tom has something to contribute to creating a lasting marriage, or I wouldn't have written them.''

''Of course.'' April looked away so he couldn't see her crushing disappointment. ''As your editor, I had no business calling you on your study no matter how I felt about your research methods. Any more than I had a right to try to change you. I was not only fighting what I thought was a stereotypical old-fashioned notion of women, but my own personal memories.''

Lucas gently wiped a tear away from the corner of her eye. ''If it will make you feel any better, April, you've made me see a side of life I seldom took time to notice before you decided to take me in hand. It may sound like a cliché, but the sun actually seems to shine brighter now. I do see the other side of the mating game—yours—so maybe your efforts weren't wasted, after all. That's why I decided to do a second, follow-up study.''

April smiled ruefully. "I have to admit you don't sound like the old Sullivan."

"I'm not." He lifted her chin and gazed into her eyes. "Look at me, April. What do I have to do to prove to you the Lucas side of me really exists?"

"I'm not sure," she said, distracted by the genuine concern she saw in his eyes. "Try me."

He looked relieved. "I have an idea that ought to do the trick. Let's make a date for tonight. It's not actually a date since I have to play tonight. I'd cancel it except that I want you to see me do what I like to do best. That ought to convince you the Lucas side of me is real. How about it?"

April swallowed the confession that she'd already seen him in action. That seeing him play the guitar, gyrating across the stage, singing, had been the moment she'd first suspected there were two sides of him. She had to give him another chance, for both their sakes. "Sounds good to me. What should I wear?"

Lucas had to stop and think. "To tell you the truth, I haven't paid much attention to what the women in the audience wear. I'm too wrapped up in the music. From what I've seen..." He snapped his fingers. "Jeans, of course." He grinned sheepishly before he went on. "Low on the hips. And, oh yeah, a flashy top with the navel showing, or something that looks like the top of a bikini."

April pretended to be disappointed. "Sounds to me as if you've been paying more attention to the women in the audience than you think. Anyway, I'm afraid I haven't got anything like that. Maybe I shouldn't—''

Lucas broke in. ''I won't let you change your mind. You still have time to go shopping.'' He glanced at his watch.

By now, April was sure Lucas had never visited a women's store, let alone helped a real woman shop. It was time for lesson five. ''Only if you come with me to help me choose.''

Lucas looked as if she'd proposed a trip to the moon. ''That's not part of my expertise. Are you sure you want me there?''

''I'm sure.'' She smiled an invitation. ''After all, I wouldn't want to look like I don't belong.''

Lucas kissed the tip of her nose. ''You're going to look great no matter what you wear.'' He took her head between his hands and kissed her again as if he never wanted to let her go. ''I have to practice this afternoon, or I wouldn't leave now. I'll be back around five to pick you up. Why don't you start thinking about some clever ideas for these debates Tom is asking for? That will keep you too busy to miss me.''

April waited until Lucas left before she turned back to the sink. This time, to stack the rinsed dishes into the dishwasher.

Debates! Her heart sank at the reminder of what Tom expected of her. She wasn't sure what Lucas's reaction to her final comments would be, or even the manner of his rebuttal. What she did know was that after spending the night with him, she couldn't bear to hurt him—even if it meant losing her job.

At least she had a shopping trip to take her mind off those damn debates.

GOOD AS HIS WORD, Lucas showed up promptly at five. "Ready?"

April eyed him appreciatively. He was wearing what she assumed were rehearsal clothes, but today's tight black jeans left nothing to the imagination. No one would have guessed that, underneath his sexy look, beat the heart of an academic.

From her own reaction to Lucas's appearance, April had an uneasy premonition that he could cause a riot among the female shoppers at Diane's, her favorite clothing store.

She took a deep breath. "I'm not really sure about this, but if my coming to the Roxy means that much to you...let's go."

When April saw the windows of the upscale women's apparel shop plastered with fifty percent off sale signs, it began to look as if her premonition might come true. Half the female population of Chicago seemed to be inside. Lucas no sooner had one foot in the door than every woman in the shop stopped in her tracks.

She knew exactly how they felt.

Lucas cleared his throat, and even as he tried to look nonchalant, he moved closer to her. "Maybe this wasn't such a good idea,'' he muttered under his breath. ''Maybe I should wait outside.''

April shook her head. ''Follow me.'' She motioned to Lucas and headed for a promising rack of jeans. To her chagrin, the largest size on the rack was not only a 4, the jeans looked as if they'd been made for under-developed young women.

She turned to speak to Lucas—and saw that he was surrounded by a gaggle of adoring teenager fans, some of who must have seen him perform. He was in the midst of signing autographs and looking over their heads in a desperate appeal for help. He seemed overwhelmed by the girls crowding around him.

Poor man. She had to save him.

Smiling, April made her way through the fans. Lesson number five was turning out to be even more interesting than she'd expected. He was not only learning about real women's lives but about the single-minded persistence of teenage girls.

Still, she came to his rescue. ''Excuse me, ladies, but I need Mr. Sullivan's advice.'' She took him by the elbow and, to accompanying sighs of envy, led him over to the rack of jeans.

Behind her, Lucas heaved a sigh of relief. ''Thanks a bunch.''

''Don't tell me you've never had fans ask for your autograph before?''

''Not in a place like this,'' Lucas answered, looking uneasily over his shoulder. ''How soon can we get out of here?''

"As soon as I find an outfit for tonight," April said as she lifted two sets of jeans off the racks. "The jeans that are designed to ride low on the hips are too small for me. On the other hand, if I buy standard-size jeans, they'll come up to my waist. As for appropriate tops, the flashy ones over there, the ones covered with sequins, have no lining. The bikini tops would hardly cover me." She gestured down at herself. "So, what do you think?"

A pink tinge came over Lucas's face as he followed April's glance at her breasts. "I'm afraid I'm the last person in the world to have an opinion on the subject of jeans, although I have noticed some that were rolled down at the waistline to here." He pointed to just above his hipbones. "As for the bikini tops, well..." He looked at the blouse April was wearing and flushed.

April smothered a knowing grin. For a man supposedly too wrapped up in his music to notice what his female fans were wearing, Lucas certainly had a lot of observations to make. As for the style and size of the tops she'd indicated, he knew enough about her figure to have known the answer.

"Well?"

"Oh, hell," he muttered. "Why don't you just get one of those shirts over there."

April grinned as she chose a pair of jeans she'd have to roll over her hips and, since she had nothing left to hide from Lucas, a see-through sequined top.

That would show Lucas that a real woman was proud of her body and had a mind of her own.

THAT NIGHT, WHEN THEY entered the Roxy nightclub, Lucas left her with a murmured request to one of the men at the door to keep an eye on her. The idea of his wanting someone to look out for her was rather sweet. The realization she was in the last place she'd envisioned herself revisiting and to still be able to take the opposite side in a rebuttal to Sullivan's article was not.

The same colored lights she'd seen before flashed about the room. A sign at the corner of the stage announced that tonight was a battle of the bands. According to the printed program, Lucas's small band was up next. The area in front of the bandstand was jammed—no room for dancing.

Soon she heard the escalating sound of an electric guitar as Lucas moved onto the stage to join his partners-in-rock. Then he began to sing, a sound almost drowned out by the calls of the enthusiastic audience. A lump rose in her throat as she realized she'd never seen Lucas look so happy.

The wonder of it all, at least to her, was why he spent so much of his time in sociological research when it looked as if he could make a living doing something he loved.

The set finally ended with a flourish. April was still trying to get her hearing back when Lucas joined her.

"How was it?" he asked as he sat beside her at the small table she claimed.

She decided not to tell him her ears were still ringing. "Great!" she answered. "In fact, I wondered how you're able to concentrate on academic studies when you enjoy performing so much."

"Family tradition," he said succinctly. "Like father, like son, but it does help to have the two sides of my personality to fall back on. I assume you had no trouble recognizing which side of me was playing tonight? Or which man I am now?"

"I'm not quite sure," April said teasingly. In truth, she saw Lucas, the man she was falling in love with. "I'd have to do a little more research of my own before I answer."

"Research," he echoed. His eyes lit up as he took in her formfitting jeans, the swell of her breasts beneath the silky fabric of her shirt. "I'm not sure what kind of research you're talking about, but since I'm a pro, I'm sure I can be of help to you. Your place or mine?"

Suddenly a little voice in April's head told her to be careful, not jump into this…thing with Lucas Sullivan. What had started out as a series of simple lessons to bring the Sullivan side of Lucas into the twenty-first century looked as if it might, given time, turn into something rather serious. She couldn't do it. In a way she'd be on probation; she'd been dumped once before by a man who'd found her lacking, and once was enough. She wasn't prepared to risk her heart again. ''This may surprise you,'' she said, ''but I need some time to think.''

''About us?'' He'd obviously sensed her change in mood and his smile faded. ''You're joking, right?''

He sounded incredulous, not that she blamed him. And for her, the realization that she was willing to take time to think about their future, instead of just walking away from him, was a surprise, too.

''No. I meant it when I told you our time together has been wonderful, but…'' she hesitated.

''But what? You have any complaints?'' He reached to take her into his arms, but she shook her head.

''No, no complaints. The problem is, I'm not anxious to change and I'm not sure you can. We're still the same people we were a few days ago.'' She pulled back and put her hand on his chest to hold him at a distance.

Lucas paused to wave good-night to his fellow band members before he answered. ''It's probably true that we wouldn't normally have been attracted to each other, but it seems we are. Maybe there is too much Sullivan in me, and not enough Sullivan woman in you. But so what? I thought we'd already agreed we weren't interested in marriage. Right?''

He wasn't quite sure why he'd ended his remarks as a question, since he was already feeling he'd never find another woman who stirred him the way April did. A woman he wanted to spend the rest of his life with.

He started to tell her so, but the sounds of the new band launching into its first number drowned him out. He could barely make out April's reply to his question, but he thought he heard her say this had to be the old Sullivan talking or he would've known the answer.

She was right, Lucas thought unhappily as he watched the change that had come over April become more evident. Clearly, she thought he *was* the old Sullivan. A man who would never have entertained the idea of marriage to an independent woman like her.

Damn! It was all his fault! He should've made sure she was convinced it was the Lucas side of him making love to her. That the private side of him had changed, even if the public side had produced "The Mating Game."

Until he could persuade April to give him another chance, there wasn't much he could do, certainly not tonight.

"I don't intend to give you up without a fight," he warned, leaning forward to speak close to her ear. "I do care for you and I'm pretty sure you care for me. It's not only last night," he added. "I know that what we have is more than sexual attraction. I know that as well as I know my own name."

But what *was* his own name now? he wondered as he looked into April's troubled eyes. Was he really

Lucas, or was he the chauvinistic Sullivan April so disliked?

He should have learned *some*thing about himself in the past few days.

He suppressed a rueful sigh. Ever since April had appeared in his life, he wasn't all that sure which man he was anymore. But he was sure of one thing. In the same methodical way he'd pursued his research, he intended to focus his attention on winning April. To make her realize she was meant for him. Even if he had to do it one day at a time.

First, however, he had to give her some space.

He drew a deep breath. "Go ahead and take the time you need to think. I don't know about you," he added as he ran his fingers lightly over her flushed cheek, "but I have the feeling this isn't going to be the end of those lessons of yours. After you've had time to think about us, I'm sure you'll realize there are still a few things *both* of us have to learn about each other."

April gazed at him wordlessly. Heartened, he went on. "I'll be seeing you soon." He gently swept a tendril away from her eyes. "There's still the debates Tom asked for, remember?"

Remember? How could she forget?

She smiled to cover the feeling that their brief relationship was ending almost before it had begun. "Yes, I remember." She paused. "I need to go home now."

Lucas would have felt a hell of a lot better about his future chances with April if her smile had reached her eyes.

Chapter Eleven

On Tuesday, Rita eyed April's choices for lunch. ''A juicy hamburger with everything on it, fries and a chocolate milkshake? Again?''

April paused in midbite. ''Why not?''

''Maybe I didn't hear right, but I distinctly remember you saying you were going to spend the weekend trying to enlighten Sullivan.''

Even though April knew she didn't have a chance of keeping the weekend's events to herself, April shrugged. ''As a matter of fact, I did.''

Rita's eyes narrowed. ''So why the need for comfort food?''

April searched for a reply that would satisfy Rita and still afford her some degree of privacy. The fewer details she gave away about the weekend and last night, the fewer details would come back to haunt her. She shrugged and took another bite of her hamburger.

Rita sniffed her disbelief. She put her lunch tray on the table, sat down and studied April for a few minutes. "I don't know about you, but if I'd spent any quality time with a gorgeous hunk like Sullivan, I would have been floating in seventh heaven. Instead, if you don't mind my saying so, you don't look at all happy."

April smiled wanly. When Rita sensed a story, she was like a bloodhound. Considering the subject of the story was not only a man, but a man like Sullivan, April knew anything less than the truth wouldn't fly with Rita. "Maybe because the weekend didn't exactly turn out the way I intended."

Rita waited while the noisy foursome from the magazine's editing department at the next table left before asking. "How did you *intend* to spend the weekend?"

"Well, I started out intending to show Sullivan the world we real women live in, but..." Her voice faded as she realized how presumptuous she must have appeared to Sullivan by suggesting he didn't live in a real world. Let alone that he didn't understand the world of twenty-first-century women. The wonder was that he'd stuck around at all.

"Don't stop there," Rita said impatiently when April paused to take a deep swallow of her iced tea. "What happened?"

April couldn't tell Rita how she'd twisted her ankle and how Sullivan had played doctor. Knowing how Rita's creative mind worked, just the words *playing doctor* would have set her off down on a road April wasn't prepared to travel. Because playing doctor meant investigating sexual differences and— She stifled that thought immediately.

''Not much.'' April tried to be casual as she told Rita about the river cruise. ''At Sullivan's suggestion, I might add. But since it fit in with my own plans, I decided to go along with him. I figured a cruise along the Chicago River would be the perfect setting to show him the mating game isn't merely a question of rational thinking. Love enters into it. I was right—love was everywhere on the cruise boat.''

Rita grinned happily. ''Now you're talking!''

''You might say the cruise turned out to be lesson number one,'' April continued, determined to keep the details to herself.

''Lesson number one? A river cruise with Sullivan?'' Rita broke into a wide smile. ''Obviously the man's not as stuffy as you thought. It only goes to show you can't go with first impressions. I mean, hey, I saw him on stage. I knew then there was more to the guy than what was on the surface. So what did you do next?''

''The company ball game on Saturday was supposed to be lesson two—a lesson in equality.'' April frowned as she recalled the indignity of being thrown off the field.

''Yeah, yeah, I was there,'' Rita said impatiently. ''We've disagreed about my pitching before and the world didn't stop spinning. That couldn't have been your only problem with the man, or you wouldn't look so disgruntled. Go on.''

"Nothing to do with baseball, I'm afraid." April took a deep breath and plunged into the details of the problem bothering her, besides the one concerning Sullivan's suggestion she could become a Sullivan woman if she tried. "I was taking Sullivan home from the game when Tom called me on my cell. He wanted me to get enough information on how Sullivan thinks so that he and I can carry on a 'cutting-edge' series of short debates."

"Debates? With Sullivan? You've got to be kidding! If it were up to me, I wouldn't be debating the guy, I'd find something far more interesting to do with him!" Rita pushed her lunch away. "Frankly, I think the debates are a dumb idea. You're good at what you do, but you've got to admit you're not in Sullivan's league."

"You're right, of course," April agreed. How could she debate a subject like the mating game from purely a personal viewpoint when Sullivan had a doctorate on the subject? "Maybe that's the trouble. Maybe that's why he was acting as if Tom's idea of a debate is a big joke."

"I do, too," Rita agreed sourly. "An exercise like that would be enough to kill any budding relationship. Tom doesn't have an ounce of romance in his soul. I swear, the man lives and breathes for the magazine. No wonder Lili can't get to first base with him. So, what happened next?"

What happened next was safe, and April told her friend about baby-sitting Paulette.

Rita giggled. "Pardon me for laughing, but that's sure a new way to get to know a man. I saw Lili this morning and she told me all about it. She says the kids are okay and back in camp until school starts again. So, go on. What happened next?"

April smiled at Rita's interest. "I gave him a rain check and we had dinner Sunday night, instead. Believe it or not, I'd actually planned to turn the night into another lesson."

Rita rolled her eyes. "Good grief! Only you would call a date a lesson!"

"I keep telling you it wasn't a date," April protested. "It all started by my trying to show Sullivan how human he is."

Rita squealed her delight. "How?"

"That a man's reaction to a woman's close proximity involves a great deal more than mind over matter."

"My theory, exactly," Rita said with approval. "So...?"

"So I knew I had to find a way to keep Tom off my back or I wouldn't hear the last of it. I thought I could show Sullivan that we could find a way to enter some kind of dialogue without cutting each other's throats."

Rita eyed April thoughtfully. "Something's missing here."

April gave up. Maybe it would help to talk things over. "I'm afraid I not only planned an intimate dinner, I dressed for the occasion. I put on romantic music and set the table with candles and wine.'' She paused when Rita's eyes widened. You're right, I overdid it. We—''

Rita's mouth fell open. ''Nah, it couldn't be. Not after the way you said you feel about Sullivan. Or should I have said *felt* about Sullivan.''

''Well,'' April said, blushing when she recalled the exquisite way Sullivan had made love to her, ''I guess you could say we became close.''

Rita dropped her tuna sandwich onto her plate and stared at April in awe. ''Are you saying what I think you're saying? You actually got *real* close and personal with Sullivan?''

April thought of just how close she and Sullivan had become. ''Yes.''

''No way!'' Rita gasped. ''Although with a romantic setup like that, I wouldn't have been able to resist the guy, either. But *you!* I can't believe you actually slept with him. One day you call him a stuffy professor who wouldn't know a real woman if he saw one and the next you're hopping into bed with him!''

''Well, he's a long way from being stuffy—it just took me a while to find that out,'' April said slowly as images of Sullivan and herself in the shower flashed through her mind. ''I not only learned a lot about him, I also learned a great deal about myself. I'm not as smart as I thought I was.''

Rita snorted. ''And you're still eating hamburgers?

I guess sleeping with Sullivan didn't show you the error of your ways, after all.''

''I didn't sleep with him! Well...not exactly.'' April glanced around uneasily to make sure no one was listening. No problem. The clatter of dishes and hum of voices left no chance of that happening.

''*How* not exactly?'' Rita persisted. ''The way I see it, when it comes to sex, there's no such thing as 'not exactly.' Either you slept with the guy or you didn't.''

''Well, let me put it this way—I didn't get a lot of sleep.''

Rita gave a great bark of laughter. ''I knew it!''

April rummaged in her purse for a bottle of headache medication. ''Please, not so loud. I have a splitting headache today. Besides, I see Arthur over there watching us, and Tiffany just came in, too.'' She popped two tablets into her mouth, washed them down with iced tea and took a deep breath. ''What I'm trying to tell you, Rita, is that I didn't sleep with Sullivan. I slept with Lucas.''

Rita leaned across the table, her eyes wide. ''No way! The last time I looked, Sullivan *was* Lucas. I distinctly remember hearing you introduce him as Lucas Sullivan!''

''I know it sounds weird, but I'm not crazy and neither is he,'' April said helplessly. ''It's as if Lucas is Sullivan's alter ego. Not only his alter ego, but a more sensuous and exciting side of him I can't seem to resist.'' April blushed. She would never be able to look at the couch in her apartment again without remembering how she'd learned it was possible for two people to share the same space. Or to be able to take a shower again without feeling Lucas's hands sliding over her, his muscular body pressed against hers and making love to her in ways she'd never believed possible.

"You saw the Lucas side of him last Thursday at the Roxy," April added.

Rita nodded. "Yes. I know what you mean. So it was this Lucas who made love to you?"

"Yes. At least I *thought* it was Lucas. When I let him into the apartment, he said he'd left his Sullivan persona outside. But now I'm not sure anymore."

Rita sighed. "Either guy would have been fine with me. So what's the problem?"

April stifled her exasperation. "The point is, I thought I was educating Sullivan."

"Educating," Rita repeated. "That's an interesting word for sex. I'll have to remember it—like the way it raises the level of what you're doing." She took a bite of her tuna sandwich while April did likewise with her hamburger. "Okay, I still don't get what your problem is. Why aren't you sure it was Lucas?"

"It was April's turn to sigh. "Well, it was something he said. Well, not what he said, but the way he said it."

Rita just looked at her.

April went on to relate how hurt she'd been when

he'd remarked on how closely she fit his idea of a perfect mate, as described in his study and article.

"No!"

"Yes. And I finally told him I needed time to think about where our relationship was headed or if there actually *was* a relationship."

"The problem grew worse," April continued, "when he went on to say that, since neither of us was interested in getting married at the moment, it didn't matter who we were. He may have put the remark as a question, but if he's not sure of himself, then neither am I."

"You had a problem with *that?*" Rita gaped at her. "I didn't think you were interested in being married! Not after being jilted!"

April smiled ruefully. "I guess I did have a problem with it. Anyway, when I have a relationship with a man, he's not going to be a 'Sullivan.' I told him I wanted more."

Rita rolled her eyes. "What more is there if you're not sure you want to get married?"

"I'm not sure, but I want more than a passing relationship or a one-night stand. So if he wants a Sullivan woman, he can keep on looking. I'm not her."

Rita reached across the table and patted her hand. "I was only kidding about either guy being fine with me, April. You're probably right. Any man who could not only write but believe in those rules of his isn't the man for you *or* me. Now, what are you going to do?''

''Well, I'm not sure I want to get into any debates with Sullivan—it only means further being involved with the man. I haven't completely made up my mind yet, but if I do, well—''

''That'll be the last you'll see of Sullivan,'' Rita said matter-of-factly. ''What a waste of a hot guy.'' She indicated April's empty plate. ''I see you ate the whole thing.''

''Yeah. But a hamburger isn't going to help this time. Anyway, Tom wants to see me. I better get going.''

AS APRIL ENTERED the elevator, she wondered what her chances would be of telling Tom she had no intention of debating Sullivan and not get fired.

She hadn't told anyone, including Rita, how much she actually cared for Lucas Sullivan. The attraction wasn't only sexual, as Rita thought, nor was it because of a subconscious search for a man with strong genes. Sullivan or Lucas, she'd actually come to love the *man.*

April punched the elevator button to the sixth floor, then stood back to savor the revelation that there was no use trying to separate Lucas from Sullivan—they were one man.

Not that she intended to do anything about it now that she knew that Sullivan wanted a Sullivan woman.

''Hey,'' Eldridge said when she walked into his office, ''the ball game on Saturday ended in a tie. How did the rest of your weekend go?''

''I suppose you could say it also ended in a tie,'' April said casually as she sank into a chair. ''What did you want to talk to me about?''

Eldridge didn't bother to check his calendar. It was obvious he'd been planning on publishing Sullivan's article in the next issue of the magazine from the moment he'd first asked Sullivan to write it. Some friend, she thought sourly.

''I've arranged for the magazine to go to press this week with 'Sullivan's Rules,''' her boss announced. ''Now, have you given any thought to the debates I asked you to do? I want to be ready when the fur begins to fly.''

April wondered if this was the right time to confess she had no intention of entering into any debates with Sullivan, or what she thought of Tom for thinking of it. ''Some,'' she replied.

''Atta girl! I know you're going to give 'em hell. Have something on my desk as soon as possible.'' Eldridge grinned his satisfaction. ''I have high hopes for the results.''

April swallowed her comment. Tom may have been talking about circulation figures, but she was thinking about Sullivan. Even if it cost her her job, she couldn't make the man she loved look like a fool, which is what such debates would do to him.

THREE DAYS LATER AND twenty-four hours after *Today's World* hit the newsstands, the magazine's editorial department recorded 782 e-mails, all but seven irate, and 123 telephone calls, six of them threatening.

"And that's *before* the flood of snail mail we're going to get," Eldridge crowed to April as he strode into her office and handed her a handwritten tally sheet.

Sullivan had a lot to answer for, April mused as she smiled noncommittally. For that matter, so did she. He, for being biased. She, for not being able to open his eyes to the real world of women. Somewhere, during the magical weekend, they each should have learned more about the mating game.

"Have you and Sullivan decided on how to go about your debates?"

She still hadn't made up her mind about whether or not she'd do the damn debates. "No, but I'm sure he hasn't had a chance to read any of the mail that's come in," she said.

"Don't forget what I told you," Eldridge said, turning to leave. "I not only admire the guy, we were frat brothers, you know. I also happen to agree with him on the subject of marriage. But the publication of his article is strictly business. A legitimate business," he repeated. "I want you to keep the pot boiling. If I know you, you'll write your debate from the viewpoint of a woman who doesn't need a man to show her how to be a woman."

"Do you have a problem with that?" April took a moment to give Tom some credit for being smarter than she'd thought he was. She was actually rather fond of Tom.

To her surprise, Eldridge winked from her doorway. "Not at all. Who could ask for anything more?"

TO APRIL'S DISMAY, RITA sailed into the office an hour later and dropped a sheaf of printed copies of e-mails on April's desk. She held a small telephone answering tape in her other hand. "You're never going to believe this, but we've had to set up a special telephone line to take all the calls pouring in! It's gotten so bad, we had to work up an automated reply."

April bit her lower lip. She'd been sure there were a lot of women out there who would take umbrage at "Sullivan's Rules," but not like this.

She actually felt sorry for Sullivan.

"I just wish I'd had the chance to go on with the lessons," she said. "Maybe things would have worked out differently."

Rita's eyes narrowed. "Don't tell me you've actually fallen for him."

April was grateful to see Arthur coming down the aisle with his refreshment trolley. She wasn't ready to share her new and tender feelings with anyone outside of Rita. Especially since the chances of anything coming of it were slim to none. She gestured to the door. "Keep it for later, Rita. It looks as if we're going to have company."

Rita glanced out the door. "Arthur?"

"Yes, Arthur. The kid shows up twice a day to remind me he's here." April sighed. "As if I could forget him. What he needs is to find someone younger and a little less naive than he is." She looked at Rita hopefully. "You don't happen to know of someone you could introduce him to, do you?"

"How about Tiffany?"

April burst out laughing. "Have mercy. I said a *little* less naive. Tiffany would eat Arthur alive."

Rita giggled. "Okay. I'm sure there's someone around. Just give me a chance to think about it." She rose to leave, but not before she blew April a kiss. "I'll take on Arthur, you think about Sullivan."

April sighed. As if she ever *stopped* thinking about him.

Chapter Twelve

April studied the new issue of *Today's World.* True to his word, Tom had used "Sullivan's Rules" as the feature-of-the-month. The cover was a cartoon drawing of a game board featuring a man and woman at odds.

No wonder feminine fur was flying.

A quick reread of the article confirmed her initial reactions to it and its author. If she hadn't had magical memories of Sullivan to fall back on, she would have been as irate as the hundreds of irate incoming telephone calls and e-mails still coming in indicated.

She had her own private ideas of what she'd include in the debates Tom wanted—if she decided to engage in them, of course. Namely, that Sullivan didn't believe in his rules as strongly as he made out in his article. And that there *was* something troubling about his rules for the mating game.

April pulled out the original copy of Sullivan's manuscript and studied it carefully, red editing marks and all. After their weekend together, she was sure she was able to read between the lines. The rules were so old-fashioned, they had to have been written tongue-in-cheek for Tom's benefit.

Maybe she hadn't been all that right about Sullivan. Maybe he had a sense of humor about himself and the subject. On the other hand, she mused as she remembered his candid remark about her having some worthwhile Sullivan traits, maybe she hadn't been all that wrong about him, either.

The realization that she'd subconsciously equated Sullivan with her former unlamented fiancé, Jim Blair, didn't help. To equate him with a man who had an ego so big that he thought it okay to leave her at the altar while he eloped with another woman was hardly a fair comparison. For starters, Sullivan hadn't proposed they marry.

Instead of the verbal attack Tom expected, she would have shown the readers the caring and tender side of Sullivan.

She reached for a ruled yellow tablet, drew a line down the center of the page and carefully listed Sullivan's mating-game rules on the left. Then, on the right, she began to list the rules as *she'd* write them.

"Can I help?"

April instinctively turned the legal pad over before she looked up. "Oh, it's you!"

"You were expecting someone else?" Rita ambled into the office.

"Not really." April smiled wryly. "I didn't want anyone to see what I was writing. Not even you."

Rita responded with a mischievous grin. "After all you've told me about Sullivan, you didn't think you could keep me out of here, did you?"

"I was hoping to." April sighed, thinking of Sullivan's smile, the little quirk at the corner of his mouth, of the way he'd bought a train for a little girl and had sat down on the floor to play train conductor. Of his heartwarming request for a glass of milk and cookies. "But I can see that was too much to hope for. Come on in and close the door behind you."

Rita did so. "You'll be pleased to know I've taken care of your request to get Arthur off your back. I put a bug in Alice Carson's ear about him. You know Alice, don't you?"

"Alice Carson? The new intern? The junior Tiffany?" Rita nodded. "How big a bug? I wouldn't want the poor kid to get hurt."

"Big!" Rita threw her arms wide. "Take it from me, that's the only kind that counts with a guy like Arthur. I made sure to tell her Arthur was too shy to approach her. I told her Arthur was stuck on her baby blue eyes and that cute little mole she has by the corner of her mouth. If I know Alice, she'll have him purring at her knees by tomorrow afternoon."

April laughed. "You're incorrigible. It's a good thing I know you're all talk and no action. Have a seat. I'll be with you in a moment."

April returned to her two lists of rules. After a few moments of deep thought, she murmured, "I don't intend to do anything about it, Rita, but I can't stop thinking about 'Sullivan's Rules.'"

"Too much thinking is your second mistake," a masculine voice said softly. "I thought we agreed that it would be more satisfying to just let yourself feel, instead of thinking about the future."

Startled, April looked up. She hadn't heard her office door open and close, but the chair in front of her desk, instead of being occupied by Rita, was now occupied by the man who hadn't left her thoughts from the first moment they'd been introduced, and Rita was nowhere to be seen. Even under the guise of a stuffy professor, he'd radiated more confidence and presence than any other man she knew. With the glint in his eyes as he smiled at her, even that persona had become more sensual.

As for allowing herself to feel with all her senses, that presented no problem. She hadn't stopped. She could still taste his kisses on her lips, hear the sound of his voice whispering words of encouragement in her ear, feel his shower-wet arms slide over her slick, wet body. Still recall the way he'd made love to her under the spray.

Nor had she gotten over the wonder that a man so dedicated to such a faulty research involving women could stir her senses in such a magical way. To complicate her thinking, in his khaki slacks and crisp white shirt open at the neck and with a twinkle in his eyes, today Sullivan was more appealing than ever.

"What was my first mistake?" April asked cautiously. She leaned across the desk to cover the legal pad with her folded arms. The less Sullivan knew about her daydreams the better.

"Saying goodbye even though we both knew we wanted to spend more time together." His deep brown eyes softened as they swept over her. "At least *I* knew I wanted more of you. Until you surprised me by saying goodbye, I thought you felt the same way."

Her mind still replaying the weekend and Monday evening, April was at a loss as to how to explain her hesitancy in continuing their relationship. How could she explain she'd thought their time together was almost over after his comment about her having potential Sullivan-woman traits? How could he have not known how afraid she was of being hurt by a man again? Or that after his playful remarks at the Roxy about not wanting to be married, she'd come to realize they would inevitably go their separate ways?

She was sure of one thing. If she didn't find a way to stop thinking about the tender and sensitive Lucas side of him, any rebuttal she might have to write would wind up being a love letter.

"What are you doing here?" she asked. "What did you do with Rita? I didn't even hear her leave!"

"In answer to your first question, I was invited." Sullivan leaned back in his chair, stretched out his legs and made himself at home. "As for Rita's leaving quietly, I didn't even have to ask. All it took was one look. She even blew me a kiss as she tiptoed out the door.''

April smothered a sigh. The romantic Rita was no better than Tiffany or, for that matter, herself when it came to being captured by the man's sensual appeal. Except, she reminded herself, at the moments when he turned into a true Sullivan.

She remembered an old saying of her father's—*the best defense is a good offense*—and decided to quit playing games. It was time to get their relationship, whatever it was, out in the open.

''Who invited you here today? Surely not Tom!'' she added without waiting for an answer. ''According to him, you're supposed to be home working on the debates, which by the way, I'm not so sure I want to go through with.''

He leaned across the desk, started to take her hand, then pulled away. ''Why not? After the night we spent together, I thought our deal was working out better than we expected—intellectual opponents in public, friends in private. Very *good* friends.''

April closed her eyes to the twinkle in his. The weekend had been one thing. Today was another story.

''We were,'' she said, ''but we're not anymore. And I told you, I don't want to do the debates.''

''I thought you'd be willing at least to talk about it.'' The corners of Sullivan's mouth turned upward in an inviting smile. ''As for who invited me over, it *was* Tom. He thinks it's only fair that I see some of the stuff that's come in."

April glanced out through the glass partition at the outer office, where a dozen women stood there glancing at Sullivan. Heaven help her, she found herself sympathizing with them.

She didn't want to meet Sullivan's gaze, but she had to. "Tom may have invited you to take a look at incoming mail, but does it have to be here, in my office? I'm trying to think."

"Sorry. I thought we could find a middle ground for this exercise."

April frowned at the way his grin turned speculative. He was gazing intently at her—or was he just looking at her lips? "With an article as faulty as 'Sullivan's Rules,' there is no middle ground, nor does Tom want one. You either believe in your article or you don't. I don't."

"Maybe, as far as debating me goes," he agreed, "but I was hoping I could explain what I really meant the other night—and hoping you'd changed your mind about us seeing each other."

April thought back to his comment that she just might turn out to be the perfect woman. Perfect *Sullivan* woman, he meant. The more she thought of Sullivan's rules for a woman to qualify as a mate, the more she realized he couldn't possibly believe she was the woman for him, no matter what he said.

"As far as I can tell," she said quietly, "there is no *us*."

"There could be," he said just as quietly. "All you have to do is give it another chance."

"*Could* is the operative word here," April replied, trying to ignore the appealing intensity of his voice. "You'll have to find someone else." She picked up a pencil. "If you're looking for Tom, he's probably in his office waiting for you. Now, if you'll excuse me, I have to get back to work."

Sullivan was intrigued by the way April tried to ignore the bond he was positive had grown between them. A bond that had no sensible definition, according to the conclusions of his study.

April Morgan might be as far from fitting the description of what she'd called a Sullivan woman as the earth was to the moon, but she was still the woman he'd fallen in love with.

He took a slow, visual inventory of her, at least what he could see of her behind the desk. He knew there was far more to her than a body most women would die for, and he desperately longed to take her in his arms this minute. Making love to April had been an experience of a lifetime. Sparring with her quick mind had been exciting, too. If he had his way, he wasn't through trying to convince her he cared for her, really cared for her, his rules be damned!

How could she ignore the powerful attraction between them? he wondered. How could she pretend not to feel the attraction? He knew she did. She blushed every time he caught her looking at him.

It was just a matter of time before something had

to change, he mused as he reluctantly rose to leave. He took a step toward her, then reconsidered. An intelligent combatant knew when to pursue and when to retreat. "See you later, teacher."

The title *teacher* echoed in April's mind as she sensed its intended meaning. There was no goodbye. He was looking forward to more lessons.

April kept her gaze on the legal pad until she heard the door close behind him. If ever there was a reminder that she hadn't seen the last of Sullivan, that parting remark had been it.

More lessons? A warmth started in her middle and radiated to points north, east and west. There was no question her body reacted to him, she thought ruefully. Only, she had a suspicion *Sullivan* intended to be the teacher this time around. How willing a pupil she'd be was another story.

The door opened and Rita stuck her head in. "Don't tell me you let that gorgeous man of yours get away from you so soon!"

"He was never mine to begin with." Feeling lightheaded, April motioned Rita inside the office. "Unless something changes," she added wistfully, "it looks as if it's going to stay that way."

"You mean the weekend was sort of a lend-lease agreement between you and it's now over?"

"I'm not sure." April sighed as she turned the yellow legal pad over. "Not that if makes a difference anymore."

After Rita left, April found herself thinking of Lucas Sullivan and their lovemaking, in bed, on the sofa, in the shower. His arms had held her to him, fitting them so closely together they'd became one. If it had felt so right to be with him then, where had they gone wrong?

Was it because she'd allowed his rules for the mating game to get in the way?

She glanced at Sullivan rule number one. "A happy relationship requires that a woman make her man feel masculine."

Opposite it, she wrote Morgan rule number one. "To make a man feel masculine, a woman needs to allow him to talk about himself."

On the other hand, and according to Rita, maybe that was what had gone wrong. They'd spent too much time talking!

April ignored the ringing of her intercom and moved on to Sullivan rule number two.

"While a man is not monogamous by nature, he is more likely to see a woman as a potential girlfriend or mate if sexual intimacy doesn't occur too soon."

April didn't buy that for a minute. Lucas had looked forward to their sexual intimacy as much as she had. Furthermore, her own brothers had married their respective college sweethearts, and there was no question they'd been sleeping together long before any vows were taken.

April thought back to how surprisingly and how quickly she and Sullivan had given in to their mutual attraction as she doodled on the yellow pad. The intercom rang again. She frowned and pressed the button. "Yes, Tom?"

Her boss's voice boomed over the intercom. "What's this I hear you won't talk to Sullivan?"

"I don't know what gave him that impression, Tom," April said as she drew a heart on the legal pad, pierced it with an arrow and sat back to admire her handiwork. "We *did* talk. You have my assurances on that."

The pause on the other end of the phone was telling. A moment later, she heard the muffled sound of male voices. Had Sullivan actually complained to Tom that she'd refused to talk to him in order to get Tom to work on her? So it seemed, she thought. She would have given a week's wages to have heard Sullivan's answers to her boss's probing questions.

Tom came back on the line, sputtering. Ignoring the yearning in her hungry heart, April interrupted him. "I have something to tell you, Tom," she said. "But it's going to have to wait until you're alone."

"Just don't forget I want your take on the debates on my desk tomorrow morning," Eldridge said. "That goes for you, too, Sullivan," he said in an aside. "I intend to personally edit the debates."

April heard the frustration in his voice. She hoped Sullivan wasn't the type to kiss and tell.

Maybe she should have sworn Rita to secrecy.

She turned back to her notes. For Sullivan's rule number three, that a woman must rein in her own desires to promote the health of a relationship, she had a ready rebuttal. She hid a broad smile with one hand over her lips while she wrote rapidly with the other hand.

Morgan rule number three: ''All a woman has to do is feed her man chocolate and he'll keep coming back for more.''

Of course, she mused happily as she wrote, there *were* two kinds of hunger. As she and...Lucas had experienced—and satisfied in a most pleasurable way—only five days earlier.

As for Sullivan rule number four—''A woman must strive for compatibility, rather than try to be sexy''—well, she hadn't needed to *try* to be sexy. At least, not during the night or the following morning, when Lucas had kept looking at her as if she were a chocolate soufflé.

April dropped her pencil and fanned herself with the yellow legal pad. She had to find a glass of cold water, or at least to take a break from thinking about the magical world where Lucas had taken her.

She glanced out the window. Where was Arthur and his beverage trolley when she needed him?

Ten minutes later, after a quick trip to the water cooler, she was back to her rebuttal exercise. An exercise that would never see printer's ink.

Sullivan rule number five: ''A woman must show her man how much she likes and appreciates him. She must shower him with affection and sublimate her own daily frustrations.''

Morgan rule number five: ''A man must do the

same for his woman. If the frustrations are sexual, a cooperative effort in lovemaking goes a long way toward sublimating them—in a very satisfactory manner. For any other frustration, a shopping trip will do.''

Her answer to the last of Sullivan's rules—''A woman must be supportive, fun-loving, easy going and generous in her praise of a man's achievements''—was much like Morgan rule number five. This type of activity should be mutual. The scene in the shower with Lucas had been ample and rewarding proof. So had the shopping trip....

By now, April felt ready to spontaneously combust. Ice water hadn't helped.

She compared what she'd written one more time with Sullivan's rules. She straightened in her chair. His article might be black letters on a white page, but now that she knew its author intimately, she wondered if his article was actually intended to be tongue-in-cheek. That he was playing a joke on his old fraternity brother, Tom Eldridge?

Then her shoulders slumped. No, she was wrong. Sullivan didn't do things lightly. His article, and the study it was based on, were dead serious.

Chapter Thirteen

April went back to scanning the rebuttal she never intended to use. She blushed to see how her own rules had turned out to be as sensual as Sullivan's. Either Rita's influence on her thinking had been greater than she'd realized, or the weekend with Lucas Sullivan had left its mark. Either way, his name was stamped all over her idle scribblings, and she couldn't keep her mind off the memorable weekend she'd spent with him.

The difference was that her lessons and her rebuttal to his rules had to do with real life while his didn't. In her opinion, marriage was about love and caring and equality and compromise, when necessary, not about rules.

Tom was going to be angry when she told him she didn't intend to play his game, but she didn't care. Now that she'd read Sullivan's rules a whole new way and compared them to her own version, she was more determined than ever not to debate Sullivan. There was nothing in her new interpretation of Sullivan's rules to suggest the mating game was a challenge between the sexes. It was more just a battle of the senses.

Had she been willing to debate, and she might have been if she wasn't in love with Lucas, she would have written that his study apparently had precious little to do with today's women finding mates. Today's women were doing well enough on their own. Furthermore, no real woman would consider following his archaic rules.

She would have gone on to say that a woman desired a stable and intelligent mate, a man whose masculinity wasn't threatened by a strong woman.

She would also have said Sullivan had either never met a real woman, or he hadn't been able to recognize one when he had.

April took a deep breath to fortify herself before she left for Tom's office to give him the bad news. There would be no debates with Sullivan; at least not between him and her.

"Coast clear?"

April let out her breath and looked up to see Rita at her doorway. "Good grief, Rita! It's five-thirty. I thought you would have gone home by now!"

"You didn't expect me to leave without finding out what you've decided to do about the debates, did you?" her friend said as she strolled into the office.

"I guess not," April sighed. "Anyway, I've decided not to do the debates."

"Have you told Tom that?"

‘‘No, but I will. I was waiting until he was alone to tell him how I feel about this game he’s playing with Sullivan and me.’’ April took off her glasses and rubbed the bridge of her nose. ‘‘I don’t mind telling you, you’re the *real* problem behind all of this.’’

‘‘I am?’’ Rita looked astonished. ‘‘All I’ve done is listen to your adventures with Sullivan.’’

April knew better. ‘‘Did anyone ever tell you that some of your outrageous ideas can be a bad influence on women like me?’’

‘‘Yeah, all the time.’’ Rita grinned and sat down on the corner of April’s desk. ‘‘That’s one of the reasons I left Texas to live in Chicago.’’

‘‘Only one of the reasons?’’

‘‘Okay, just one. Add my mother to a gaggle of well-meaning older brothers,’’ Rita said with a shrug, ‘‘and since I’m the baby of the outfit, every last one of them worries about me and tries to run my life.’’

Arthur appeared in the doorway before April could commiserate with Rita. ‘‘Excuse me, Ms. Morgan. I just wanted to say good night….’’

‘‘Good night to you, too, Arthur. Anything else?’’

Arthur’s face turned pink. ‘‘I also wanted to thank Rita.’’

Rita winked at April before she answered. ‘‘For?’’

‘‘For…for Alice,’’ he stammered.

‘‘Glad to be of help,’’ Rita said as Arthur backed out of the office.

April hid her laughter until Arthur was out of

sight. "How did you manage to get Arthur and Alice together so quickly?"

"I can't take all the credit," Rita said modestly. "Like I told you, it's all about reminding two people who like each other to do what comes naturally. Like in the real mating game," she added.

"*Your* version of the mating game, you mean," April said wryly.

"So how did things go between you and Sullivan this afternoon?" Rita asked. When April shook her head, Rita said judiciously, "My advice to you is not to give up yet. It ain't over till it's over. Forget about what Tom wants and do what comes naturally."

"Doing what came naturally wasn't the problem," April said as she recalled just how naturally close she and Sullivan had become.

"Well, good luck," Rita said as she rose to leave. "Whatever you have in mind, I have a feeling there's still more to come."

"Not when all Sullivan and I do seems to drive us further apart," April said wistfully.

Rita held back. "That's because the two of you talk too much. And like the man said, according to what I overheard, both of you need to let yourselves feel, instead of talking and thinking so much. It sounded as if the two of you were doing okay before you started to analyze each other. Take my advice, there has to be something that brought you together in the first place. All you have to do is find it."

April gazed at Rita with a new understanding. Underneath that flamboyant facade lurked a wise woman. Rita could be right. She had found a lot to like about Lucas Sullivan before. ‘‘You could be right,’’ April said softly.

Rita waved goodbye. ‘‘Thank goodness I’m not the one who’s falling in love. Anyway, it’s time to go home and feed Lucinda. That dratted cat chews on the drapes if I don’t come home and feed her on time.’’

April hurried to hug Rita. ‘‘Thank you for your advice. As for Lucinda, why do you keep her if she’s so demanding?’’

‘‘Because she loves me and I love her,’’ Rita explained. ‘‘It’s hard to lose someone you love, even if they drive you crazy. See you tomorrow.’’

Rita was too much on the mark again for comfort, April thought as she watched Rita waltz off down the hall. She turned to look out the window at the winding Chicago River and wistfully recalled the lesson on love....

TOM ELDRIDGE GLANCED up in surprise when April knocked on the door. ‘‘You beat the clock, April,’’ he said with a broad smile. ‘‘I didn’t expect to have your notes for the debates until Monday morning. I was just about to leave, but as long as you’re here, have a seat while I look over what you have.’’

April drew a deep breath. ‘‘Tom, I came here for another reason. I haven’t made any notes.’’

Tom exploded. ‘‘What do you mean you don’t

have any notes? What have you been doing for the last few days? I know you and Sullivan have been together at least long enough for you to come up with a few ideas on why his beliefs are wrong!''

''True, but I've decided I'm not qualified to challenge a respected academic like Lucas Sullivan.''

''Hell, that's what an editor is for!'' Eldridge snorted. ''Why do you think I hired you?''

''I know it's my job to suggest possible changes,'' she said, her own temper rising. ''I tried to, but you wouldn't let me. Don't worry, since you went ahead and published his article, you'll have plenty of opinions to use on your letters-to-the-editor columns. I don't see a problem.''

''Well, I do! I wanted something that would feed the readers' frenzy!''

''Seems to me you have it. Pick someone else to help to raise circulation if you want to,'' she shot back. ''I would have come up with a middle ground, anyway, not a back-stabbing exercise.''

Eldridge leaned across the desk. ''Listen to me and listen carefully, April Morgan,'' he said slowly and deliberately, enough to raise the hair on the back of April's neck. ''When it comes to boosting circulation, there *is* no middle ground in this business. We either make it big or we don't continue to publish!

''Hell,'' he added as he ran his fingers through his hair, ''I learned that truth at my father's knee and I learn it all over again every damn month. We've been skating too close to the edge of profitability too long. When it comes right down to it, publishing Sullivan's article has not only been good for the magazine, it's been good for you and Sullivan, too.''

April had to keep from balling her fists. What was he saying? Good for her and Sullivan in what way? As sparring partners...or intimate partners. Lovers.

''Just what *did* you expect?'' she asked at last. ''A blow-by-blow description of just how friendly Lucas and I became over the weekend?'' she continued before she could stop herself. ''Is that what you wanted? So I could use it against him in order to show him how flawed his thinking is?''

Eldridge's anger turned into a nod of approval. ''So it's 'Lucas' now, is it?'' he said as he looked approvingly at her. ''Good. My answer would have been yes, as long as you kept it in good taste. It'd be great for sales. Of course,'' he added before she had a chance to tell him what she thought about his lack of taste, ''we have to remember large numbers of our readership are unmarried, independent women. Like you,'' he added with a look April wasn't sure indicated approval. ''All you had to do is to remember how you reacted the first time you read Sullivan's study and put it in writing.''

''How could I forget?'' April asked bitterly. ''For your information,'' she went on, too angry to care what she was saying, ''that's what I tried to do. I encouraged him to talk about himself. I even made him my specialty—chocolate latte. I became friendlier than I ever imagined I could be with the chauvinist he turned out to be. Just like you!'' When her boss's eyes widened, she wanted to bite her wayward tongue.

But Eldridge just smiled, took her by the arm and gently urged her to the door. ''Take it easy, April. I wasn't telling you how to do your job. It was only a suggestion. Why don't you go home and relax. No matter how things turn out with Sullivan...'' His words trailed off.

April left with the sinking feeling that she couldn't trust Tom to do the right thing. Was her boss referring to the cutting-edge debates he'd asked for? Or, as an old friend and frat brother of Lucas's, was Tom intimating that she and Lucas were meant to be together? It was clear that whatever Tom had in mind, the right thing might be wrong for her.

AFTER SPENDING AN uncomfortable weekend reading irate snail mail and printed-out e-mails, Lucas arrived at Eldridge's office at nine Monday morning.

''Great!'' Eldridge beamed as he welcomed him into his office. ''Now that you've had a chance to read some of the mail blasting your article, I expect you have plenty to say in reply.''

Lucas shook Eldridge's hand, wondering why, from the elated expression on the editor's face, he'd ever agreed to defend his study. As far as he was concerned, while there might be room for argument, his work didn't need defending. ''That depends.''

''I don't mind telling you the mail is still coming

in,'' Eldridge said jovially. ''Apparently the word about your study has spread. I understand sales are going through the roof!''

''Happy to have been of help,'' Sullivan said dryly. ''Not all of the letters are negative, I hope?''

Eldridge looked complacent. ''A few are favorable,'' he said, ''but it looks as if the majority of our female readers would like to have you tarred and feathered. Have a seat.''

Sullivan dropped into a chair and rubbed his forehead in frustration. ''As I told you when you asked me to write the article, my conclusions are based on several years of empirical research. I say so in the article. Why so many of your readers have taken offense beats the hell out of me.''

''That's because the magazine is not an academic or scientific publication. Our readers are primarily middle-class professional women.'' Eldridge picked up a copy of the current issue of the magazine and paused to admire the cover. ''Looks great, doesn't it?''

Lucas scowled. ''It looks more like something out of a comic book.''

''It gets the idea across.'' Tom laughed. ''My father, the founder of the magazine, wisely decided to publish diverse articles of contemporary interest. I'm happy to say your article has attracted a greater interest than most of the others we've published.''

Sullivan felt a spurt of anger. At Tom for setting him up, at April for not insisting he take another look at his manuscript and at himself for allowing her attraction to get in the way of objective thinking. He should never have agreed to Tom's debate idea.

It was his fault for succumbing to Tom's flattery in the first place, he thought angrily. Although, if he'd known just how controversial the study would become, he would have made Tom pay through the nose for the privilege of publishing it.

Eldridge frowned when he finally noticed Lucas's empty hands. "And now to your rebuttal to those letters. You did draft one, right?"

Sullivan shook his head. "No, I decided there wouldn't be any point to it. After I had a chance to read the samples of mail you gave me, I realized there was very little I *could* say that anyone would listen to. Instead of a rebuttal, I've decided to do a second, follow-up study."

Eldridge's eyes lit up. "A follow-up study? I hope you intend to have us publish the conclusions. At a higher rate, of course," he added quickly when Sullivan frowned.

"Maybe," Sullivan said noncommittally. "However, as long as I'm in so deep, I might be persuaded to make a single exception—one comment and no more. But not before I read April's comments."

Eldridge frowned and rubbed a hand over his chin. "That makes two of us who want to read them. Hell, I wish I had something of hers to show you. All I do have to go on is what she did say when she was bawling the hell out of me."

The look on Lucas's face grew hard. ''What exactly did she say?''

''Uh, well...'' Tom glanced at him, and his face reddened. ''It's just that...well, it just seems wiser to keep what she said to myself.''

''Tom...'' Lucas said warningly.

Eldridge gave in. ''If I tell you, I'd like to keep it between us.''

''That bad, was it?''

Eldridge's flush deepened. ''You'll know better than I do, but she said something about baby-sitting together, chocolate lattes and becoming more friendly than she intended....''

Lucas's gaze hardened. ''Are you sure she said that?''

Tom shifted uneasily. ''Hell, I would have thought you'd be pleased. I didn't tell you this before, but I asked you to write the article not only for the magazine's sake, but to bring you and April together.''

Lucas gasped and surged to his feet. ''You make one hell of a cupid! My advice to you is to stick to the publishing game and leave matchmaking to someone who knows how to do it.''

''I swear, I didn't mean to hurt anyone,'' Eldridge protested. ''I knew there's more than one side to every behavioral theory, your mating-game study and article included. I just didn't know the two of you would take the whole business so seriously.''

''I don't know about April, but *I* intended to have my study taken seriously!'' Sullivan reached for his wallet and pulled out the check Eldridge had given him on Friday for the article. ''I decided not to cash this until I spoke with you this morning. And now...'' he tore the check in two and then put the pieces of paper in his pocket. ''As a matter of fact,'' he added as the idea of April's evident betrayal angered him more and more, ''I'm beginning to believe the publication of my article was nothing more than a scam the two of you cooked up only to boost your magazine's circulation! I wouldn't have expected you to be so unethical, Tom.''

''Come on, now,'' Eldridge protested, his face mottled with anger. ''There wasn't anything unethical about it. Your article was published exactly as you wanted and you know it. Sure, I thought it was a good idea to get you and April together, and a damn good way to increase circulation. After I tried it on April, her reaction made me sure of it. Hell, that's what the publishing business is all about!''

''Publishing my article was one thing. Asking April to engage me in a series of what she called lessons is another!''

''Lessons?'' Eldridge frowned. ''I don't know squat about any lessons. A friendly exchange of debates, sure,'' he blustered. ''From the way April reacted to my raking her over the coals by sounding off about the two of you, I'd say the exchange went well beyond any lessons. Hell, she seems to have fallen for you.''

Sullivan scowled. "That part is none of your business!"

"Sure, but to give April her due, before you go off half cocked, I think you ought to give her a chance to tell her side of the story."

"Why? As far as I'm concerned, anything having to do with the publication of my mating-game article is done, over, finished. As far as April goes, that's a no-brainer. I'd have to be deaf, dumb and blind not to believe the two of you planned this caper together!"

"Not true!" Eldridge protested. "You're a fraternity brother of mine and April is my employee. We're all family around here. You might not think so, but I do care what happens to her and to you, too. As I've told you, I was hoping to get the two of you together."

Sullivan surged from his chair. "You should have stopped to think about that before you called her after the ball game and urged her to become involved with me so we could get into a 'cutting-edge' debate! Hell, I think April's lessons were your idea, too!"

Eldridge took a cautious step back. "Look, I don't know anything about any lessons. But if they have anything to do with chocolate, that's your business, not mine."

"I'm not sure I know what I'm talking about anymore, either," Sullivan muttered as he turned to leave. The thought that April had betrayed him with words was secondary to the realization she'd betrayed him with her body.

"What I do know," he said "is that I let myself be fooled into believing April had good intentions in this exercise. I'd actually begun to believe..." His words trailed off.

Eldridge followed him to the door. "If it'll make you feel better, Lucas, let's forget the debates. I hate like hell to say you're right, but it looks as if I have something to prove to you. I'll use a stock reply for any incoming mail. Or I'll think of some other way to get a rise out of readers." He paused. "You might not believe it," he went on, "but I am sorry things turned out this way."

"So am I," Sullivan said, disillusioned with himself and with Tom—as well as with the special woman he'd found and lost in April. "Maybe April was right about me and my work, after all. Maybe there's no such thing as a Sullivan woman today."

"Perhaps not," Eldridge conceded, "although I have to tell you, considering that I spend my working hours trying to stay ahead of strong women like April, that I meant it when I said I agree with your theory—the woman you describe in your study is the only type of woman I think I could live with. So if you do happen to find one that fits the description, be sure to let me know. I'll marry her myself."

Chapter Fourteen

Muttering to herself, April was busy packing up her desk when the door to her office opened. She glanced up to see the last man she wanted to see right now. "You!"

"Yeah," Lucas said. "Why surprised? We did agree to meet again to talk about our debate." He crossed to her desk. "Now seemed as good a time as any. Although—" he frowned as she dropped a small stack of yellow lined legal pads into the box "—you look busy."

"Take it from me, this is not a good time," she answered, and added pens, pencils, a ruler and a stapler to the box.

Sullivan glanced around April's office. Framed covers of the magazine had been taken off the walls, the bookcase was bare. The plaque honoring her as the employee of the month was facedown on her desk.

"Moving day?"

"You got it," she muttered as she added several books. "I'm about to quit."

"Don't you think you should quit first, then pack up?"

She glared at him. "What do you want?"

Wordlessly, he opened his hand and two small pieces of paper fell onto her desk.

They looked suspiciously like two halves of a check, and April was taken aback. She wasn't sure what was behind the gesture, but it didn't take a genius to know that Lucas was angry and had just made a statement.

"Is that what I think it is?" she asked warily. "The check for the article Tom asked you to write?"

"You got it!"

April fingered the pieces of paper. "Then I suppose the question I should be asking is, why have you torn it up?" She sensed his answer would involve her, and her heart took a dive.

"Because I can't take money for something I consider a serious effort when it's apparently a joke around here! Hell, I must have been nuts to agree to write the article for Tom's magazine in the first place. I should have realized you and Tom set me up."

April felt herself blanch. Her relationship with Sullivan had been a case of two steps forward and three steps back from day one, but this was too hurtful. She shook her head. "You're wrong. If anyone should feel they've been set up, it's me."

"Really? Why don't you tell me just how wrong I am?" he said in a voice that sent cold shivers down her spine.

"You must have spoken to Tom before you came in here," she said as she eyed the torn check. "He has to be the one who set you off."

"Any reason for me not to be angry after what he told me?"

"He must have told you I refused to go along with the idea of a debate."

"Yes, as a matter of fact, he did. He also added a few more interesting details."

April's worst fears were realized. Tom's anger or being fired she could live with. Lucas's reaction to her impulsive outburst in Tom's office Friday was something else. The cold look in his eyes was enough to freeze hell.

"I'm sorry. I was so angry at Tom I lost my cool and said things I never meant to say. I was trying to reach a middle ground in the debates, but Tom wasn't interested."

His gaze hardened. "There wouldn't have been a middle ground. I've said it often enough—I stand by my research. What I don't appreciate is having been set up!"

"Come *on!*" April protested. "I told you from the outset that the debates were Tom's idea and were intended to increase magazine circulation. And no matter what he said he wanted, surely you must have understood I wanted our debates to be tongue-in-cheek."

"I'm a sociologist, not a mind reader, Ms. Morgan," he answered tightly. He began to pace in front of her desk. "And I don't play games when it comes to my professional life. I don't have a quarrel with differences of opinion, not even yours. What I do have a problem with is your telling Tom about our weekend together. I was under the impression it meant as much to you as it did to me."

"It did," April said when he paused to take a breath.

She still tried to put his anger in perspective. If he was that hurt by Tom's gloating about the weekend she and Sullivan had spent together, that made two of them.

"I might have said more than I should have when I sounded off to Tom," she explained, "but I'm darn sure that whatever he inferred and then told you was his imagination working overtime."

April rose, walked around her desk and poked Sullivan in the chest with a manicured finger. "As for your article, you not only wouldn't listen to me, you fell for Eldridge's good-old-boy flattery! Even though it was obvious, at least to me, that he had something more in mind for your article than its publication. As for our relationship, if that's what you want to call it, you don't have to worry about it anymore. It's over!"

Sullivan's anger might have been softened by his

reluctant admiration of the fire in April's eyes if he hadn't noticed the sheet of paper April had on her desk near where the two pieces of his check had fallen. Most people didn't realize his experience as a teacher enabled him to read upside down, or April would have made an attempt to hide it. Even upside down, it was clearly a bill for services rendered.

"A bill from Alexandra's Catering Service?"

April lunged for the bill, but he was too fast for her. He picked it up and read it aloud. "'Lamb-and-vegetable kabobs, rice and salad for two.'" He looked at her incredulously. "For last Sunday night, right? And here I thought you made dinner." He snorted. "We didn't eat much. Maybe you should ask for a refund."

April felt herself color. "I only said dinner was ready. I never said I cooked it. Besides, the bill is my business, not yours."

"It's my business if the dinner was part of the scam you and Tom cooked up!"

"I'm sorry you think so," April retorted. "Give that back to me." She grabbed the bill out of his hand. "And while I'm at it, I might as well tell you since the dinner made you think of me as a potential Sullivan woman, I regret having ordered it."

"If that's how you feel, then at $175 the dinner was overpriced." He reached into his pocket and took out his wallet. "I'll pay my share."

"Put your wallet back in your pocket!" April said

angrily. ''Finding out how you actually feel about me is worth every penny.''

Sullivan looked taken aback, but April hardened her heart. This was the second and last time she intended to have her heart broken. At thirty-two, she should have known better.

''In retrospect, I don't suppose you'd have made love to me if you hadn't believed I made dinner,'' April said, fighting back tears. ''I don't apologize for not knowing how to cook. For your information, the truth is, the only thing I know how to make is damn good chocolate latte.''

She poked him in the chest again for emphasis, hard enough to get under the opening in his shirt and to meet his bare skin. A big mistake. The shower scene flashed through her mind. She snatched her finger away.

''As long as we're talking about guilt,'' she went on, ''I might as well confess I'm also guilty of trying to show you a warmer, more inviting world than the one you'd been living in! And furthermore, Mr. Sullivan, *you,* not me, made the first move that night. Although, to be honest, I know I reciprocated. I was only doing what my friend Rita says comes naturally—I thought I was making love with you.''

''April,'' Sullivan interjected. ''Can I say something?''

''No. I'm not finished yet! I once made the mistake of trying to be the woman my ex-fiancé wanted me to be. I must have given you the same impression.

But get this straight. I'm not and never will be a Sullivan woman!''

''Are you finished yet?

''Almost,'' she sputtered. ''I just want to go on record that I don't need a man to make me feel like a woman!''

He regarded her warmly. ''You definitely feel like a woman.''

April ignored the warmth in Lucas's eyes. ''Good. Now, unless you have something else to say, we're through.''

''I'd say we're about even,'' he said. Even though he should have remained upset by April's sounding off to Tom, her distress reawakened the tenderness he'd felt for her. A tenderness coupled with a desire to bring a smile back to the face of the woman he'd fallen in love with.

As he watched April trying to collect herself, Lucas began to suspect she'd managed to turn the tables against him. He'd come to her office to tell her what he thought of her, to call it quits and move on. Instead, as he gazed into her stormy eyes, he found himself wondering what he had to do to get into her good graces again.

He even began to suspect April was more right than wrong about him. To his surprise, he found himself grateful that the debate exercise had come up to force this confrontation and clear the air.

With the cards on the table now, he was beginning to see himself as April saw him. A man who didn't have the sense enough to let a woman make him whole.

Surely, that woman had to be April, he thought as he saw tears form in her eyes. He wanted to take her in his arms again, to tell her he loved her, to ask her to forgive him for being an ass. He wanted to be skin to skin, heart to heart with her. To share a narrow couch, a bed and a shower. He wanted to taste her, smell her skin, hear her sighs as she found her pleasure. But now was not the time.

It wasn't going to be easy, he knew as his eyes locked with April's shiny ones. One way or another and step by step—the methodical way he did his research—he intended to use everything he'd learned in the past week to convince her they belonged together.

"Apparently I don't know myself as well as you know me, sweetheart. A pity," he said slowly, resisting the temptation to wrap her in his arms. "Given the right time and the right place, I think we can be good together. Even if your answer turns out to be no, at least we will have given ourselves time to think about where we're headed, if anywhere at all. In spite of what I told you about your thinking too much, it does give us space. Before I go, I want to tell you you don't have to quit the magazine to prove your point. I don't know about Tom, but *I* got the message. Who knows...?" He left the thought unfinished and turned to leave.

April watched Lucas go, his words wrenching at

her heart. He'd sounded as if he was asking for a truce.

Maybe it was too late for them. She and Sullivan had been unable to communicate their innermost thoughts until now, yet the closer they seemed to come, the farther apart they seemed to grow.

Not that she wanted Sullivan to walk out of her life, she thought, swiping at her tears. She'd have to figure out if they were headed anywhere. But not before making it clear she wasn't a Sullivan woman.

And not before he showed her he'd changed.

April turned back to the window overlooking the Chicago River, leaned against the window frame and studied the cloud formation that drifted across the sky. Once burned and determined not to be burned again, maybe she *had* been overly sensitive. Maybe she should have spent more time educating herself at the same time she tried to educate Lucas.

"April?" a tentative voice sounded at the door. "Is it all right for me to come in?"

April's frown changed to a smile as she turned to greet her friend, Lili Soulé. "Yes, please, come in," she said, then gave her a warm hug. The magazine's graphic artist, Lili possessed a creative spirit, but she had the pragmatic mind of a Parisian and the romantic soul of a woman who had loved and lost. A woman who was ready to love again.

Gazing fondly at her friend, April found it difficult to understand why Tom, Lili's secret love, hadn't fallen head over heels for her.

"Last week and today, I swear that everyone in the office has found an excuse to walk in here." She laughed. "I was beginning to wonder when it would be your turn."

Lili blushed. "It is true then, this, what I hear from Rita? You and this Mr. Sullivan have formed a *tendre,* or as you say in this country, an attachment for each other, and have broken it now?"

April managed a shrug. "That's more or less true. I'm afraid he might be too much of a Sullivan man for me. You saw the ridiculous article he wrote for the magazine."

"Oh, yes," Lili agreed. "I also remember you were much annoyed with him. You said you were going to straighten him out by educating him to the world we women live in. This is true?"

"I was annoyed with him and, yes, I tried to educate him," April agreed with a wry grin. "Before I was through, though, I'm afraid I turned out to be a sucker for velvet-brown eyes and a man I thought needed me."

"This is Sullivan?" Lili's eyes grew wide.

"The brown eyes, yes. As for needing the real me, I think he's just now realized who I am and isn't sure what to do about it."

"Oh, April. Maybe he will come around, as you say."

"Only if he gives up thinking I have the potential of becoming a Sullivan woman—you know, a woman who needs a man to admire, to care for and, according to Sullivan's study, sublimates herself to his needs. I go along with wanting a man to care for, but not the rest of his rules."

Lili sighed. "This is not such a bad thing, April. A woman needs to give something of herself to a man before she can feel like a woman. My mother told me this is a woman's nature. It makes her want to bear a man's children."

"Do you think that giving something of yourself to Tom will work that way? After all, he's as big a chauvinist as they come."

It was Lili's turn to shrug. "He's also the most charming man I know. When he visits the studio, I see a loneliness in his eyes. I also see the hidden soul of an artist. And, like your Mr. Sullivan, I think he needs a woman to care for him in order to be able to change.

"Tom Eldridge? No way," April countered as she recalled her boss's devotion to business. "Tom may be a gruff bear of a man on occasion, but he's a workaholic with dollar signs for eyes. No wonder he's never taken the time to marry."

Lili's expression turned pensive. "From what I hear, he will have to marry someday to make his father happy, I think. I hear his father wishes to become a grandfather before he dies."

To April, seeing Tom Eldridge as a husband and a father was crazy. Lucas, on the other hand, did have a softer side to him.

One interesting thought led to another. Lucas, an

only child, had a living father who, like Tom's, exerted a strong influence on him. An influence that only a strong woman could overcome.

Maybe Lili was more right than wrong. Maybe both men needed a loving, caring woman to show him how to recognize and enjoy the real world.

"I think you have something there about Tom," April said thoughtfully. "He needs to be married to a real woman, instead of the magazine. And a couple of kids to keep him too busy to always think about work. The way I see it," she added as her gaze swept Lili, "we'll have to come up with a way to get his, and maybe Lucas Sullivan's, undivided attention."

Lili looked interested. "How do we do this thing?"

"Easy," April said with a greater confidence than she felt. "We'll talk to Rita. I think it's time for another one of her sermons on relationships."

"What is this sermon?"

"Wait and see. Come on, it's time for lunch. Let's go downstairs to the cafeteria and find her."

"I HEARD YOUR GUY TANGLED with Eldridge this morning. It looks as if he must have followed up that argument with you," Rita said after April explained her mission. "It's getting to look like an epidemic of lonely hearts around here."

April laughed. "It sure looks like it. That's what we're here to talk about. I was so angry I would have quit if Lucas hadn't told me I didn't have to get my point across. You're right about the argument Lucas had with Tom. He actually tore up the check Tom gave him for the article and dropped the pieces on my desk. I told him off, but I'm afraid I'm having second thoughts."

Rita nodded wisely. "And you, Lili?"

"April brought me here," Lili said, and looked around to make sure no one was listening. "Something about a lesson regarding men."

"With me as the teacher?" Rita asked. "Why me? I'm the only one around here without a fella."

"Come on," April said as she shifted restlessly. "You've been full of advice about what you think is the actual truth behind the mating game. Was it real or was it all talk?"

"I wish," Rita said. "As a matter of fact, I'm beginning to believe I need some comfort food more than you do. You, at least, have your man."

"That's the point," April said. "I'm not sure I *do* have Sullivan."

"And I do not have Mr. Eldridge, either," Lili joined in.

"Now, that *is* a problem," Rita agreed, "but maybe the solution is easy. As long as you keep thinking of him as Mr. Eldridge, you're never going to get him to notice you. In my opinion," she went on, "all you have to do is look him in the eyes and speak to him as an equal. Once he realizes you mean business, he won't be able to resist you.

"And as for Sullivan," Rita added, "that's easy,

too. All you have to do is to quit thinking of the man as being two men and concentrate on him as being Lucas. If you need any reminders,'' Rita said with a wink, ''just go to the Roxy and watch him play.''

Chapter Fifteen

Two nights later, after considering Rita's advice, April found herself in the audience at the Roxy. The place was packed as usual. She wore snug, brand-new jeans, a misty-green T-shirt that fit her like a second skin and new boots. A last glance at the security mirror that hung over the door confirmed she fit right in.

Lucas was on the stage playing his guitar and singing. He wore his signature black leather pants and black shirt, only tonight the shirt was buttoned to his throat. His eyes were closed. The sight of his long fingers dancing across the guitar strings sent shivers through her. She imagined them on her skin.

April could tell by the closed expression on his face that Lucas was singing the words by rote, playing by memory. Maybe she was the only one who could tell the difference, but something about him told her his heart wasn't in his music and that his mind was somewhere else.

If he was the reason for her heartbreak, then surely she must be the reason for the change in him.

She thought back to the recent heart-to-heart she'd had with Rita. Her friend had actually withdrawn her "it's all sexual attraction" theory. A mutual sexual attraction was fine, she'd finally confessed, and in fact, desirable. But when it came to thinking of actually spending the rest of your life with a man, there had to be a lot more. Genuine liking and respect, for starters. Something about the person that made you easily imagine spending the next fifty years with him.

Sullivan!

In the telling, April realized Rita had given away the secret of why she was still single. In spite of her flamboyant theory about sexual behavior, she was saving herself for the right man to come along, just as she and Lili were.

As for Lili, April had no doubts she would eventually get her man.

And so would she.

She remembered an old saying, "something about taking the first step to get where you want to go."

She knew she had to be the one to take that first step tonight, or she would lose the man she loved.

Lucas ended his song and, amid applause, turned to the audience and asked, "Any requests?"

"'Coming Home to Love,'" April shouted impulsively. It was the song Lucas had written and sung to her after she'd made him a chocolate latte that memorable Sunday night. A song that reminded her of how much she loved him.

The other band members glanced questioningly at Lucas. He straightened, shaded his eyes and glanced over the audience until he saw her standing there, her hands folded over her heart, a smile on her face. His expression changed. He'd seen her.

"'Coming Home to Love' it is," he said, smiling broadly. He turned to the other band members. "Follow me, guys," he said, and began to strum.

Slowly, achingly, Lucas played the introductory notes of the song that, along with the man who sang it, had stolen April's heart. The bass guitarist and drummer joined in.

His eyes never leaving April's, Lucas began to sing the lyrics of a man longing for the woman of his heart to come home to. Then, as the music grew more joyous, he sang of his happiness when he finally finds her.

Just like the first time he'd sung the song to her, April's heart swelled with love for Lucas. Her heart ached anew as she heard the yearning in his voice, saw it in his eyes. The same yearning that grew in her.

Suddenly Lucas put down his guitar and moved to the edge of the stage. The band kept playing the melody as he gestured for her to join him, holding out his hand to her.

April knew from the look on his face, that Sullivan's rules had fallen by the wayside.

She reached the stage and extended her arms to him. He leaned down and pulled her up onto the stage and into his arms. The audience came to their feet and cheered.

"Shall we take this somewhere more private, sweetheart?" he said with a wave to the audience. When she nodded, he lifted her in his arms and, to thunderous applause, he carried her offstage, out through the stage door and into the starry night.

He set her on her feet and began to kiss her, passionately, thoroughly. Eventually he pulled his head away and gazed into her shining eyes. "Whatever you have in mind for where we're headed, sweetheart, I'm with you all the way."

"What about Sullivan's rules?"

"Forget them. I like you just the way you are. Don't change a thing. As for me, well, we can work on that together until I get it right. More lessons."

"I think you already have most of it right," she murmured into his seeking lips.

He drew back. "Whoa. Hold on there. Don't you think you're being too supportive and generous in your praise of my achievements? That's Sullivan's rule number six, by the way."

She laughed. "That's okay, because I'm making up for it by breaking rules three and four. I'm doing nothing to rein in my desire and being shamelessly wanton in my behavior." She kissed him on the lips. "Let's go home, Lucas Sullivan, and get started on lesson number six."